Pilgrim's Descent

A JOHN PILGRIM NOVELLA

MITCHELL MEDFORD

Blue Sky Fiction • Orlando, Florida USA

Blue Sky Fiction, Publisher
11310 S. Orange Blossom Trail, Suite 197
Orlando, Florida 32837
www.blueskyfiction.com

Publisher's Note: This is a work of fiction. Names, characters,
places, and incidents are a product of the author's imagination.
Locales and public names are sometimes used for atmospheric
purposes. Any resemblance to actual people, living or dead, or
to businesses, companies, events, institutions, or locales is
completely coincidental.

Book Layout © 2015 BookDesignTemplates.com

Pilgrim's Descent / Mitchell Medford. -- 1st ed.
ISBN-13 978-0-9909492-5-1
ISBN-10 0990949257

CONTENTS

Welcome to Paris_____ 1
Chapter 1 _____ 5
Chapter 2 _____ 12
Chapter 3 _____ 16
Chapter 4 _____ 23
Chapter 5 _____ 30
Chapter 6 _____ 33
Chapter 7 _____ 38
Chapter 8 _____ 44
Chapter 9 _____ 49
Chapter 10 _____ 53
Chapter 11 _____ 58
Chapter 12 _____ 63
Chapter 13 _____ 71
Chapter 14 _____ 75
Chapter 15 _____ 83
About the Author _____ 89

Welcome to Paris

"This will be the largest sale of military weaponry in the history of our organization," the beautiful, dark-eyed woman whispered as she toyed with her food. "It is conditional upon your agreement to a face to face meeting with Charles. He insists upon it."

"Tell Charles Aragon to come here to Cairo," Dieter Heilberg offered for about the tenth time with a heavy German accent. Even after two decades of living in the Middle East, he tended to lapse into his native dialect when he was tense. "He knows I cannot risk setting foot on European soil. Interpol would have a field day if they could lay hands upon me."

"He has the same problem. In our line of business, we rarely make friends, but we definitely make enemies. The Syrians and the Turks are particularly eager to put his head on a pike," she countered. "I have tried my best to change his mind, yet he will not complete the deal without a personal interview."

Heilberg glared at the ravishing woman across the table with a mixture of exasperation and lust. This is why he loved French women and despised French men, he reminded himself. The females were intoxicating, and the males all needed to be exterminated!

Her name was Melina Chartres, and she was the most capable weapons broker he had ever met. Heilberg had also never met a woman he wanted to bed more than Melina. He would have traded both of his Egyptian wives and perhaps a body part to sleep with her. But, what she was proposing was never going to happen; he would not—could not—go to Paris!

As a Muslim convert and committed jihadist, Heilberg was responsible for several attacks in France, Denmark, and his abandoned homeland of Germany. He was on the Interpol top ten list of most wanted terrorists, and his capture would surely mean death or life in prison. He was not amenable to either of those possible futures.

"This is insufferable," he blurted within the confines of the private dining compartment. "I have already put enough money on deposit to operate a mid-sized country for a year. Assure Aragon I can protect him here. I have a small army at my disposal." He reached past her glass of wine and stroked the back of her hand with his index finger. "Enough of this dreary talk. Let's go to your hotel and make love."

The woman closed her eyes and gasped just a little at his touch. She said in a husky voice, "You know I cannot have a relationship with an active client. Charles won't permit it. But, sweet Dieter, if we can conclude our business together..."

She let the tantalizing possibilities hang in the air.

"He just wants to keep you all to himself," her aroused companion snarled. "Is he screwing you?"

Melina drew her hand away. "That is disgusting! He is my half-brother, and he is very strict about our business behavior."

"A seller of death with a code of ethics—how schizophrenic is that?"

"Now, you are just trying to be ugly." She took the linen napkin from her lap and placed it beside her plate. "If you will have your driver return me to the hotel, I will inform Charles that you wish to terminate the arrangement. He will refund your deposit, less the mandatory twenty percent surcharge, of course."

Heilberg knew he could not let the weapons get away. His partner, Imam Jabbar, had to have them to mount the offensive in Afghanistan. There was neither the time nor resources to put together the collection of armament Aragon was offering.

Melina could see the hesitation on his face and she said, "Dieter, my darling, you have not been on the radar for Interpol or the French authorities for two years. Paris is so romantic in the spring, and I live alone in my apartment."

Two days later, Heilberg called Melina on her private number and made arrangements for the meeting. He could hear the excitement in her voice. After all, closing a deal worth a quarter billion dollars can be a powerful aphrodisiac for a girl.

His people arranged to buy all of the tickets on the Qatar Airways flight from Cairo to Charles De Gaulle Airport. They placed local business people and their families with travel visas in the seats. The passenger manifest was also laced with several of Heilberg's security guards that had been allowed to carry handguns aboard. Airport security at Cairo International was intelligent enough to accept a healthy gratuity to look the other way.

When the aircraft landed in Paris, everyone stayed in their seats as they had been instructed to do. Two of Heilberg's armed agents departed first, and shortly, one of them came back and nodded to his boss indicating the way was clear. Heilberg patted the petite flight attendant on the bottom as he exited the plane and followed his man up the ramp to the terminal.

Melina was waiting for him in the reception area beyond the off-ramp cord. She was as lovely as ever in an orchid-colored mini-dress and calf-high boots. Standing beside her was a man in a handsomely tailored suit who he recognized as Charles Aragon. With his dark hair and trim moustache, he looked more like a banker than a purveyor of heavy military weapons. Although he had never met him before,

Heilberg knew him from the plethora of photographs his agents had taken on various occasions.

He wondered momentarily if Aragon was aware how thoroughly he had been vetted before this meeting. The arms dealer's reputation was impressive, but to quote a former President of the United States, Ronald Reagan: "Trust, but verify."

As he approached his hosts, Melina gave him a beaming smile, but it was her half-brother who stepped forward to extend his hand. Heilberg clasped the offered palm vigorously.

"Welcome to Paris," said Charles Aragon.

Immediately, two ticket agents at the nearby gate counter whipped out pistols and leveled them on the security guards accompanying Heilberg. A swarm of men came rushing from various directions, all with guns drawn.

It was a trap! After all of the checking and cross-checking, Heilberg realized he had been duped into a damn trap! In a panic, he turned and sprinted back toward the jet way. If he could get aboard, his two armed men could hold the passengers and crew as hostages. He would have bargaining chips to be traded for a trip to freedom.

As he reached the entrance to the ramp, he noticed the cute flight attendant to whom he had bid an overly familiar goodbye. She was blocking the way with all of her 110-pound frame, but that is not what stopped Heilberg dead in his tracks. In her hands, she held a deadly-looking assault rifle pointed directly at his chest.

Chapter 1

The Al-Areesha Restaurant is well positioned on Imam Al Adham Street in Baghdad, and it offers a menu of authentic Middle-Eastern cuisine that goes beyond the ubiquitous kabab. Western tourists who are looking for American food can find plenty of fast food outlets in the Green Zone, but if one is ready to go native, Al-Areesha is the place to dine.

John Pilgrim had glanced at the choices, but he was waiting for two other people and was content to sip on a cup of hot chai tea. He was sitting with a view of the street and taking note of the other customers and the parade of passersby on the busy boulevard. To an untrained observer, John would have seemed to be almost disinterested in the people around him, but in truth, he could have recited a detailed description of every person who came within his vision. It was what he was trained to do, and he had practiced the routine for so many years that acute situational awareness was second nature to him. The skill had saved his life more than once.

His job as the regional chief for an international counter-terrorism network called Alliance Base often placed him in life threatening missions. Sometimes he played the role of a kind of vigilante cop; other times he worked undercover as a covert operative. He was also the supervising handler for a dozen secret agents, but basically, John Pilgrim was a spy, and he had been one for a large chunk of his adult life.

He had put himself through college with part time jobs and some supplemental support from the ROTC program of his school. The tuition money was helpful, and after graduating with a degree in American History, he owed the US Army a four-year stint as a second lieutenant. Fairly quickly, John's aptitude propelled him out of the infantry and into Army intelligence in Afghanistan, and while he was still in uniform, he was approached by the CIA. He transitioned almost seamlessly from looking for spies to being one.

John saw Melina as soon as she stepped out of the woman's dress shop across the street, and his heart skipped a beat. She knew he would be watching and flashed him one of her brilliant smiles. She performed a runway turnaround for him in the doorway of the shop to show off the outfit she had chosen. Her dress was a sky blue silk that covered her from throat to ankle. She wore a white scarf over her head, and although only her face and hands were exposed, John thought she was the most beautiful thing he had ever seen in his life.

Melina caught a break in the traffic and hurried across the street. He stood up as she approached the table, and they kissed each other conservatively on the cheeks. This was Iraq, after all, and public displays of affection were considered scandalous.

"Still no sign of Al?" she asked as they sat down.

"No, but we knew he might not be able to get here," John answered. "It's not like he can just ask the boss for a day off." He squeezed her hand resting on the tabletop. "You look exquisite, by the way."

"Thank you, sir. I dressed just for you, and may I say, you look especially handsome in your gray suit. The blue tie makes your eyes glow."

Even though he was crazy in love with the girl, he was still a bit self-conscious whenever she complimented his appearance. John had reverted to his natural hair and eye colorings after vacating his "legend" as Charles Aragon. It had been over two years since they had put the terrorist Dieter Heilberg into a French prison, yet he occasionally missed the dangerous and handsome persona of the rich arms dealer. Aragon was special, but when he looked in the mirror these days and saw the clean shaven face, the light brown hair, and the pale blue eyes, he felt ordinary. It was a constant wonder that the stunning woman next to him had agreed to become his wife.

"I makes me a little sad no one we love will be here to see us get married," Melina said "It is bad enough our parents are gone, but we have to keep the most important day of my life secret from all of our friends, too."

"I'm sorry, sweetheart, but you know it is the only way we can protect our jobs," John placated. He caught his breath and frowned. "Do you not want to do this?"

"Oh, no, you don't, monsieur," she scoffed with that adorable French accent. "We are getting married today, and don't you dare try to weasel out!"

"Can't I leave the two of you by yourselves without this constant squabbling?" asked a voice behind them.

"Al!" Melina cried joyfully. "You are here—I am so glad!"

She jumped up and threw her arms around the newcomer and kissed him vigorously on both cheeks. John stood up as well, and when Melina had finished mauling their friend, he shook Al's hand firmly.

His full name was Mohammad Ali bin Omar al-Ahmad, and he was a CIA agent imbedded under deep cover with an Iranian terrorist group called *Mujahidin al Islam*—loosely translated as "the holy warriors of Islam." The jihadists were commanded by a zealous Shi'ite imam named Jabbar, and he operated with impunity inside Iran while he conducted attacks on Western interests throughout the Middle East.

Mohammad Ali willingly responded to the nickname of Al, for he loved the two people in front of him. John was not only Al's handler in the Company, they were also best friends. As a Sunni Muslim in league with the CIA, he was risking his life just to be present today.

"I think you may be slipping a little," Al said as he joined the pair at the table. "You were unaware that I was standing behind you."

"Sorry, but I saw you; I just didn't want to spoil your surprise," John grinned and pointed to a glass partition directly across from the seating area. A ghostly reflection of the party was displayed in the glass.

"Of course, no matter the occasion, you are always on duty," Al chuckled. He produced a smallish box bound with a gauze bow and handed it to Melina. "This is a little something I found in a shop in Tehran."

"Al, you shouldn't have," Melina squealed. "Can I open it now?"

"Of course, if you must, little bird," her friend conceded.

She slowly unwrapped the gift, relishing the moment. A very fine piece of Qatar porcelain in the form of a tiny bowl with a matching lid was inside the box.

"Oh, my, how lovely!" she exclaimed. "Look, John, how pretty this is!"

"I know you will be unable to wear your wedding bands except when you are alone," Al explained. "I thought perhaps it would give you comfort to know that your rings were joined together in this little bowl, waiting for you."

"It is a perfect gift. Thank you, Al," John said. He glanced at his watch. "It is time to go; we cannot keep the minister waiting."

John left a generous tip at the table to compensate for taking up the space without ordering a meal. They walked to a four-door Toyota in the adjoining parking lot, and for the sake of convention, Melina got into the back seat. Al took the passenger seat. The drive to the Christian church took only a few minutes even with busy city traffic.

Al turned in his seat and said to Melina, "I still find it confusing that a Roman Catholic can marry a Baptist without repercussions. In Islam, Sunni could never marry Shia; it would mean certain death for both."

"My priest and John's minister would probably frown on this union, but Christians let Christ sort it out," she explained. "In fact, the cleric who will marry us today is neither Catholic nor Baptist; he is Coptic."

They arrived at the church which was situated between two commercial businesses. The building was small and very old, and there were no signs to draw attention to the fact that Christians worshiped inside. John parked on the street, and they entered the sanctuary through the front door. The priest was waiting with six of his parishioners—three men and three women—to bear witness to the marriage ceremony.

Because he spoke only a few words in English, the minister greeted John in Urdu. Fortunately, John was fluent in the native language, and even Melina had a fair understanding of conversational Urdu. The ladies took Melina aside and offered their blessings and assisted her in using the tail of the head scarf as a veil to cover the lower part of her face. Likewise, the men drew John and Al to the other side of the altar and shielded their view of the women. The priest came over to accept the gold wedding bands from John and to lead the group in prayer.

The ceremony was simple and short, and at the end, John unclipped Melina's veil so he could kiss his bride. He gave the priest a nice contribution for the poor box, and the wedding party departed amidst numerous blessings and well wishes. As they drove away from the little church, Al offered his own blessing to the marriage.

"I pray that Allah will grace your union with children as smart and beautiful as Melina," he said.

"What about me?" John asked with mock injury. "Surely, I have some attribute that would be a blessing to my offspring."

Al made a face as though in deep thought. He nodded, "Yes, may your children be as lucky as their father to attract mates so far above their station."

Melina snickered from the back seat, and John grouched, "Nice, very nice indeed."

"Where shall be go for our wedding dinner?" the bride asked.

"I would love nothing better than to spend the evening with you, but I dare not," Al sighed. "I need for you to drop me off at a truck depot at the edge of the city. I have been promised a ride that leaves for Iran in about three hours. I cannot afford to risk Imam Jabbar becoming suspicious by being absent tomorrow morning."

"Is there a place to eat at the truck stop?" Melina queried.

"Yes, but it is scarcely wedding fare, and you are too overdressed for a truck stop," Al said.

"It isn't the food or the place that is important," John countered. "It is the company we share it with."

Thirty minutes later, they were chatting over plates of chicken and rice with the faint odor of diesel fuel as an ambience. They ignored the sidelong glances from the rough and tumble customers that frequented the eatery. John's smart phone rang, and when he looked at the caller ID, he frowned and answered the call at once.

"Wait a moment until I can get to a private place," he said to the voice on the phone.

He excused himself and went outside to sit in the Toyota. When he returned a few minutes later, he had a grave expression on his face. He sat down heavily in his chair beside Melina.

"What has happened?" she asked as her own face clouded with worry.

John leaned forward confidentially and whispered, "He has done it, just as he promised he would. Dieter Heilberg has used his wealth to bribe enough people to engineer a prison break. He has escaped to parts unknown."

Chapter 2

The news about Heilberg had temporarily dampened the mood on their wedding day, and the newlyweds had bid Al good bye on his 700 kilometer journey back to Tehran with a sense of trepidation. At his sentencing, Heilberg had not only promised to break free from prison but also to exact the ultimate revenge on Charles Aragon and Melina Chartres. However, even such dire threats were not sufficient to ruin their wedding night.

The couple spent the next day and night in their hotel suite as well and only ventured out briefly the following day for brunch. After the meal, they decided to abandon their plans for a tour of the city and hurried back to the room instead. Unfortunately, on the third morning, they had no choice but to pack up. Melina was due back in Paris for a staff briefing with the French counter-terrorist unit of Alliance Base.

John ordered breakfast through room service and had just finished his shower when the food arrived. He accepted the cart in his bath robe and strolled back into the bedroom. He removed his robe and was wearing only a bath towel tucked around his waist. Melina eyed his half-nude body appreciatively. She was covered only by the top sheet with her dark tresses cascading over her pillow.

"Would you like to eat in the sitting room, or shall I serve you breakfast in bed?" he asked.

Melina ignored the question and remarked, "I don't think I can walk. I feel like I have been ravished by a bull."

"Be careful what you start, young lady," he cautioned with his hands on his hips. "You have time for food or sex but not both. So, which is it?"

His bride drew her legs up and covered her privates with her hands in feigned terror. "Blessed Mother, protect me from this sex machine!"

He went to the serving cart and pulled it next to the bed. He sat on the edge of the mattress and fed her bites of frittata and fresh melon, chased with sips of orange juice. Melina was naked, but she had tugged the sheet up and tucked it demurely under her arms. When she had her fill, she indicated she was finished, and John rose and moved the cart away from the bed.

As he turned back, he saw that Melina had tossed aside the coverlet. She stood up and stretched languidly like a cat awakening from a luxurious nap. Her stunning beauty and sexual power took his breath away.

"I'm going to take my shower now," she said, strolling toward the bathroom. She stopped at the doorway and looked over her shoulder. "You should come. You look like a dirty boy to me."

John dropped his towel on the carpet and followed her into the bathing area.

Afterward, there was no time to spare. John jumped into his clothes and packed the carry-on luggage while Melina busied with her hair and makeup. They elected to take a cab to the airport, so they would not be hampered by parking the car. When they arrived at the gate, passengers were already lined up for boarding.

Melina was not scheduled to return to Baghdad for a week, and suddenly, seven days seemed like an eon. They held onto each other until the last possible minute. Melina swiped a tear from her cheek and kissed her husband one last time before boarding.

"Call me every night," he told her. "I will count the hours each day until I can speak to you."

She hurried onto the aircraft before they closed the doors. John stood at the windows and watched as the jet taxied away from the gate, until it rumbled down the runway, and until it lifted into the sky and disappeared. He had never felt so miserably alone in his entire life.

In a twisted way, it was a blessing John had Heilberg's escape to deal with. It kept his mind occupied on tracking down the dangerous villain instead of obsessing about his absent wife. His counterpart with Alliance Base in France reported that two of the prison guards complicit in Heilberg's escape had been captured and aggressively interrogated. They had revealed everything they knew, which was very little. The helicopter that airlifted Heilberg off of the prison roof was crewed by members of the terrorist's own Egyptian security team. The guards had overheard that the final destination for the escapee was Iran, but they no idea how or when he planned to get there.

John was sure the only reason Heilberg chose Iran was because, for the proper sum, the Ayatollahs would not extradite him, and he could also renew his relationship with Imam Jabbar. Once he gained access to his vast funds, he would be in the market for weapons again, and that meant a lot of Westerners, especially Americans, would begin to die very soon. It was imperative to get a message to Al to report any news, however slight, on the whereabouts of Heilberg. If the criminal's

...location could be pinpointed, several options would become available to take out the terrorist.

For his own part, John remembered that his quarry had relatives—wives and children—in Cairo. It was a longshot, but he intended to head up a surveillance team to watch the man's family. Due to her extensive knowledge about Heilberg and his motives,

Melina would be a perfect fit for the team. He convinced himself he was not simply rationalizing an excuse to have his wife with him while a monster who had pledged to kill her was on the loose.

He discussed this possibility with Melina that very evening when she called him. She agreed it was a great idea. John had instructions for Al placed in a dropbox in Tehran. Within 24 hours, he had pulled together his team, and they were strategically positioned in Cairo. Another day later, Melina joined him, and for the first time since he had watched her board the flight to Paris, John could breathe a little easier.

His new comfort level was short lived. The following afternoon a black SUV drove by the apartment house where Heilberg's two wives lived. Without warning, gunmen in the vehicle opened fired on three members of the daytime surveillance team. A female operative with 10 years on the job was critically wounded in the attack.

Obviously, Heilberg had set up a surveillance unit of his own, only the instructions were to eliminate any agents that presented a perceived threat to the wealthy terrorist's family.

Chapter 3

With the element of secrecy blown, it was an easy decision to take Heilberg's two wives, three sons, and a daughter into custody. John leaned on the diplomats in the US embassy to convince the Egyptian secret service to hold the terrorist's family members in a safe house under heavy guard. The strategy was to use them as bait to draw Heilberg from Tehran to Cairo, but after several days, John realized the possibility of luring him out of Iran was futile. The escaped prisoner would not repeat the mistake of being trapped a second time.

On the other hand, Heilberg's henchmen were not so fortunate. The CIA team went after Heilberg's security team covertly without notifying the Cairo cops. It took three days of rousting all of their contacts and snitches, but they finally got a lead on three of the shooters from the SUV. They were holed up in a house with a small arsenal of weaponry and a suicide vest for each of the assailants.

John led the assault team himself, going in just after dark to take out the bad guys. Melina was stationed in an unmarked van parked close by to coordinate team movement and handle communications. The team caught Heilberg's soldiers by surprise and disposed of them before they had a chance to blow themselves up. Not only were the dead jihadists wearing jackets wired up with C-4 plastique, but also a big drum with an LED panel squatted in the middle of the room. To his horror, John realized it was a huge bomb rigged for detonation by remote control.

"Get out of the house now!" John shouted to the three team members of his assault team. "We have been set up!"

As the agents scrambled to exit the death trap, John heard Melina's voice in his ear.

"You have an SUV moving toward you from the north end of the street!" she warned. "Take cover!"

The team cut across the path of the oncoming vehicle searching for places to shield themselves. They barely made it to the other side of the street before a horrendous explosion demolished the house and sent a blinding flash high into the night sky. John had just taken shelter behind a car parked at the curb. Instinctively, he rolled away from the vehicle as he heard the boom. The concussion lifted the car into the air and tossed it onto its side at the exact spot that John had occupied a moment earlier.

Even as burning debris was falling all around the bomb site, the SUV came roaring into the breach with the windows down. The occupants began firing automatic rifles at the partially exposed agents, and one of John's teammates was cut down. He and his people returned fire as the black vehicle sped past. Recklessly, the van containing Melina and her driver wheeled from the curb to the middle of the road to block the way. The SUV rammed the passenger side of the van without braking and crushed the panel.

With the grill and hood of the SUV ruined, the driver threw the gear into reverse and tried to back out of the battle zone. John and his two remaining agents peppered the vehicle with withering fire, and the driver of the fleeing vehicle was struck in the throat. The SUV rolled to a dead stop in the street, and the agents cautiously approached the stalled automobile. Suddenly, it seemed too easy.

"Stop! Don't go near it!" John hollered into his throat mike as he backed away searching for a new shield.

The SUV disintegrated in another explosion that rocked the neighborhood. A piece of the engine block was hurled forward like a burning projectile, and it struck the damaged communications van and embedded deep into the side.

"Melina!" John cried in panic, as he sprinted toward the smoldering van.

"I am okay," his bride's voice crackled. "We got out of the truck in time."

John found her a few yards beyond the wreck tending to her injured driver, and he scooped her into his arms. At that moment, he did not care who saw they were more than just teammates. The thought of losing her was more than he could bear.

"John, I'm not hurt," she whispered in his ear. "Take care of the rest of the team."

Reluctantly, he released her and hurried back to see to his men. The agent that fell during the initial barrage from the SUV was dead from multiple wounds in the chest and head. A second man was suffering from a painful flesh wound in the upper thigh. Melina reported through his headset that the van driver had suffered a broken shoulder from the crash. John notified the controller on duty at the CIA facility about the dead and wounded, and within 30 minutes an ambulance was on the scene to whisk away the disabled operatives. Those who were not injured had been told to disperse before the authorities arrived.

He and Melina spent the next hour dealing with the Cairo police concerning the tremendous damage caused to an Egyptian residential area. The gruesome remnants of an estimated six suicidal terrorists added greatly to the displeasure of the local cops. Nonetheless, the two Alliance Base operatives were ushered away as soon as the news media showed up. The police had no intention of explaining why foreign counter-terrorist agents were operating with impunity in Egypt.

As soon as they were told to leave the scene, they walked to John's car parked two blocks away and drove to the hospital to check on the wounded agents. The van driver was a French national named Henri Basha, and his fractured shoulder had been wrapped and immobilized. He had been treated and released. The agent that caught a bullet in the thigh was an American CIA operative like John. His name was Doug Folsom, and although the gunshot missed the femoral artery, he had been admitted overnight for observation. The deceased agent was an Iraqi named Naheed Malik, and John did not relish the call someone would need to make to the mother of the twenty-five year old hero.

There were reports to be filed with the section chief in Langley and the French director of the Alliance Base operation in Paris, but those discussions could wait until the next day. When, at last, they left the hospital, John took Melina to their hotel room. They showered and made love and fell asleep in each other's arms. When Melina woke up, her husband was not in her bed. She trundled into the sitting area and found him making coffee with the in-room brewer.

"What time is it?" she murmured. "And why did you leave me?"

With her dark hair tousled in ringlets about her face and her eyes still heavy with sleep, she looked more like a little girl than a battle-hardened covert agent. John continued to be amazed by how much he adored her.

"It is far too early for you to be up, and I did not leave you. I came in here to make you coffee," he said, and to prove it, he placed a steamy cup on the table—black with three sweeteners, the way she liked it.

She slumped into a chair and cupped her hands around the heated mug and watched while he made himself a cup, black with no sweetener.

"What are we going to do about this?" she asked quietly.

John knew exactly what her question meant, because he had been stewing over the same issue. They were in a dangerous line of work, and although they were married, they could expect lots of time away from each other and a tremendous amount of worry about their respective spouse's safety.

"I think we should consider retiring from the spy business," he declared, as he joined her at the table.

"That is easier said than done; we can't simply turn in a letter of resignation," she responded. "Besides, don't you really mean I am the one who should quit?"

"No, absolutely not," he said. "I have been an undercover agent for 15 years, and I suddenly realize I have been waiting for you to come into my world for a lot longer than that. I am ready to open a new chapter of my life with you, and if it means closing an old one, so be it."

"You are so dear I could eat you up," she sighed. "I have been catching bad people for five years, and I still think the job we do is vital and important. We are the thin line between peace-loving people and the monsters that want to kill them. In good conscience, I don't know if we can walk away from that responsibility."

"My darling, I agree the work we do is essential, but every time we take down a terrorist cell, another one pops up like weeds in a garden. The need for covert operations will continue long after we are no longer active field agents. Don't you want a chance at a normal home and family?"

"Of course I do! It's just that we have been through a terrible event, and we should not make big decisions like this until we get some distance from it. Let's discuss this later when our perspectives aren't clouded by emotions."

"My perspective is clear as a bell," he said as he folded his hands in surrender. "If anything should happen to you, I am done anyway, so why not be done with it before something happens?"

Melina came around to his side of the table and wriggled her way into his lap. She kissed him on the temple and said, "Nothing is going to happen to either of us. Someday, you are going to regret your wish, because I will be fat with sagging breasts, and you will have five snotty kids to deal with."

They dressed and had a light breakfast before checking on Doug Folsom at the hospital. The charge nurse reported he was running a fever, and the doctor had decided to extend his hospital stay for a few days.

Before it was time to make their reports to the two controlling agencies, they developed a proposed plan of action for locating and neutralizing Dieter Heilberg. The attempt to use his family and draw him to Egypt had failed, so a more direct approach was called for. They needed to move the base of operations back to Baghdad and develop a strike team. It was a sure bet Heilberg would offer to make another arms deal for Jabbar. As soon as Al could confirm the two terrorists were together in Tehran, a surgical strike could be launched to take them out.

There was a seven hour difference between Cairo and Langley which meant John could not make contact with his section chief, Mike Kinsdale, until later that afternoon. Since there was only a one hour difference with Paris, the report to the French counter-terrorism unit could be conducted right away.

At ten o'clock, they called Marcel Renault, the Alliance Base director for France and the Middle East. As expected, he was furious about the results of the mission in Cairo. Not only had the operation resulted in the death of an agent and serious wounds for three others, the double explosions had already created a diplomatic firestorm with the Egyptian government.

Melina took the lead to try and defuse the conversation. "Monsieur Renault, the mission eliminated six of Heilberg's key people in Cairo, and we have isolated his family so he can have no contact with them. We have also developed a plan to pursue Heilberg when he arrives in Iran."

"I do not want to hear about any further plans," Renault interrupted. "I want you on the first flight back to Paris. I intend to place you on administrative leave while we investigate last night's disaster."

Chapter 4

It took ten minutes to convince the French director to calm down and listen to their plan. At last, he agreed to suspend his order to recall Melina until after John communicated with his CIA supervisor. The deciding factor was John's assurance that the US agency would bear virtually all of the expense of the proposed covert operation.

As soon as the conversation with Renault concluded, Melina looked hopefully at John and asked, "Do you really think the Company will underwrite the costs of another initiative?"

"I don't see why not. I have an operating budget at my disposal," John answered. "However, Kinsdale holds the purse strings, and he could always override me."

"That is a great deal less than the guarantee you just gave to my boss," she said. "If this does not work, I may be ready for a domestic life a lot sooner than expected."

They spent the rest of the day working out the details of an action plan. John identified a dozen agents that could be drafted for surveillance and direct action in Iran if the need arose. He also sent a secured email to the agent who was charged with the duty of sending and receiving mail messages with Al via a dropbox. The operative was a native pharmacist named Mahmood Qadir who owned a drug store in the oldest part of Islamabad, Pakistan. An hour after John sent his email he received a reply from Qadir.

They had ordered lunch in the room, and while Melina set up the table, John summarized the message for her.

"Al says there has been no appearance of Heilberg, but he is certain Jabbar has been in touch with him. The imam called in all of his top commanders for a high-level meeting, which is something he has never risked before. Al reports there will be a major initiative in Islamabad within the next few weeks, but he does not know what the target is."

"When was the message written," Melina asked as she motioned for him to join her at the table.

"Two days ago," he answered. "It is possible we are already behind the curve on this."

At precisely four o'clock, John placed a secured call to Mike Kinsdale, the section chief of covert operations in the Counter-Terrorism Center. Melina was careful to be silent to avoid any awkward questions about her presence in the room.

"Mike, I need to move my operation to Pakistan to be ready for a new offensive by Jabbar's Mujahidin al Islam," John said with his opening volley. "And, we need to cover the lion's share of the expenses so I can draft my Alliance Base agents into the plan."

"Okay. No problem," Kinsdale agreed without hesitation.

"That was unexpected," John said. "What has happened?'

"About four hours ago, our consulate in Lahore, Pakistan, was attacked by a suicide car-bomber. We lost two marines on duty when it blew a big, damn hole in the front lobby of the building. Within 30 minutes, Jabbar was talking to a reporter at Al Jazeera claiming credit for the bombing."

"I see Dieter Heilberg's fingerprints all over this. Jabbar is going to obtain the weapons and munitions to create all manner of havoc with the German's un-limited resources."

"So, what do you intend to do about it," Kinsdale demanded.

As soon as my man in Jabbar's inner circle gives me a location, I plan to take Heilberg and the imam out the same way Seal Team Six took care of Usama bin Laden."

"Get your team set up in Islamabad, but do not go into Iran without authorization from me. Are we clear on that point?"

"Roger that," John responded.

Immediately after the call ended, another was placed to Marcel Renault. The Alliance Base director's attitude was much improved from the one he had displayed earlier in the day. The news about the American consulate had reached Paris, and when John confirmed that the CIA would be absorbing the cost of the extended operation, Renault was almost giddy. Before the sun set below the horizon, John and Melina were en route to the capital of Pakistan.

Within a few days they had set up a base of op-erations in the bustling Jinnah Market of the city. This put them close to the pulse of the population and separated the team from the scrutiny of the foreign diplomats in the embassy conclave. Melina drew in a half dozen agents under the aegis of Alliance Base, and John recruited an equal number of assets that were connected to the CIA.

The team trained and planned, but the days dragged into a couple of weeks with no jihadist activ-ity occurring in Islamabad and no actionable intelligence forthcoming from Ali. As expenses piled up, the controller in Langley began to question the viability of continuing the mission. Likewise, the di-rector at Alliance Base suggested that other pressure points required reassignment of the team's person-nel.

John was deeply concerned about Al; several urgent messages to the secret dropbox in Tehran had gone unanswered. The silence meant that either the embedded agent was under close observation, or worse, he was compromised and possibly dead.

Mohammad Ali had been a vetted member of the Holy Warriors for more than three years and had risen quickly through the ranks to become a second-tier lieutenant among the mujahidin. The Company had constructed a seamless identity for Al, based mostly upon his true life experiences. As far as the jihadists were concerned, Al was a Shi'ite convert from the Sunni faith who was committed to the destruction of the West. Nothing could be farther from the truth.

Al had been raised by his uncle, Akbar, following the murder of his mother and younger sister when Al was barely seven years old. It was a ruthless Shi'ite raider named Jabbar that had led the attack on the mostly Sunni Iranian village as religious cleansing sanctioned by the Ayatollahs. The mayor of the town and all males above the age of eight were lined up against a wall and shot to death. The women and children had been herded into the local mosque just before Jabbar gave orders to destroy the building with a fire bomb.

If Al had not been visiting Akbar on that day, he would have been among the slaughtered. From his earliest memories, the boy was primed by his uncle to someday avenge the death of his family. He had grown into manhood totally dedicated to the destruction of Jabbar and all of his followers.

John had been Al's handler in the Company for two years, but they had been friends for much longer. During a fierce battle with a Taliban raiding party in Afghanistan, John had been seriously wounded and unable to walk. Al had rushed to his side to hold off the enemy and then carried John on his shoulders a quarter of a mile to safety. They had become like brothers in the ensuing months and years, and the prospect that Al's cover might be blown was devastating for John.

At last, three weeks into the mission, Qadir, the pharmacist, reported he had retrieved a lengthy report from the dropbox. As John had suspected, Al had been under tight scrutiny. Jabbar had offered him as an assistant to Dieter Heilberg. For almost a month, he had served mostly as a bodyguard for the Islamic convert and warlord.

That evening he and Melina read through the report again.

"Al is certain an embassy will be the target of a major attack, but he doesn't know yet which one or when it will occur,' Melina summarized. "He seems fairly positive it will not be the US embassy."

"Security has been doubled on all of our facilities since the incident in Lahore," John said. "Jabbar will choose a less risky target."

"I don't mean to sound callous, but providing surveillance to prevent an attack on an embassy is really secondary to our primary mission," she said. "Neither Jabbar nor Heilberg would risk being personally involved in a local bombing."

"No, of course they won't, but the Company has tied our hands about making an incursion into Iran," he replied. "We are totally dependent on Al to provide an exact location for these devils before we can get a green light to go in-country."

"When you say 'the Company,' you really mean Mike Kinsdale. Is there any way you can go over his head?"

"Sure, if I want to be removed from field assignment and stuck on a desk in Virginia. Anyway, it would be futile to take a strike team into Iran without exact coordinates. According to Al's report, the two leaders never spend the night in the same place twice."

"What are we going to do, John? Both of the agencies are going to pull the plug on this operation if we cannot produce results very soon."

"I know, darling. We can't keep waiting on Al to provide a solution. I have an asset in Lahore. She owns a dress shop there, but she is also plugged into the jihadist network. I am going to drive there in the morning and gather whatever information she has. I will be back tomorrow night."

John departed before dawn, and true to his word, he was back in time for a late supper with his wife. Melina had prepared a home-cooked meal with lighted candles on the table. The aroma of spice and sandalwood filled the apartment. She met him at the door in a pretty dress with a couple of martinis in her hands.

"Wow, what a surprise!" he exclaimed "If this is the reception I get when I leave for a day, perhaps I should go away more often."

"Yes, it would give me time to take care of my other lovers," she quipped as she guided him to the table.

They made the small talk of newlyweds over a chicken casserole and tossed salad. After dinner, she led him to the couch with cups of coffee.

"I have some news," she said.

"So do I," he added.

"Let me hear yours first," she directed as she smoothed a small wrinkle from her skirt.

"The scuttlebutt among the jihadist underground is that Heilberg just moved his entire operation into Tehran, and Jabbar is in the city, too," John said. "They rarely met together in person, and when they do, it is very brief. However, if we can lock in on their separate locations, two small strike teams could hit them simultaneously and terminate the leaders."

"It still sounds like a long shot to me," Melina said.

"Yes, I know it does," he conceded. "We remain dependent on Al to provide the timetable." When Melina did not respond, he asked, "Now, what is your news?"

"I went to the doctor today," she said quietly.

"What is wrong? Melina, are you sick?"

"No, sweetheart, I'm not sick. I am pregnant," she gushed. "About 12 weeks."

"Pregnant! Darling, that is wonderful," John rejoiced. "Wait—we have only been married for 12 weeks."

"That is right, you big stud. You knocked me up on our wedding night."

Chapter 5

During the next several days, the euphoria of prospective parenthood was tempered by intense discussions concerning Melina's retirement from field service. Their private time away from the team became debating sessions in which John pleaded for her to resign her position with Alliance Base, and Melina countered with assertions she and their child would never be safe until Dieter Heilberg was either in custody or dead. The issue reached a decision point when another message was received from Al.

"Heilberg has made a deal for a huge shipment of weaponry," John read from the report. "This will give Jabbar the recruiting tools he needs to put together a sizable fighting force to invade Afghanistan. At all costs, we have to have to find a way to prevent the delivery of those arms."

"The only way to do that is to take Heilberg out of the picture," Melina said. "He is the one with the contacts and the money. Without his help, Jabbar will be back to kidnapping tourists and suicide car bombings."

"Our best chance to accomplish this may be coming up shortly," John responded as he studied the end of the handwritten message. "In the meantime, Jabbar plans to attack the Danish embassy here in Islamabad. He intends to retaliate against an editorial published recently in the *Jyllands Posten* newspaper. The article memorialized two Danish reporters who were beheaded in Afghanistan, and the writer repudiated Islam as a false religion of hatred and death." He tapped the sheet of paper with excitement. "Here is our chance! Two days after the assault, Heilberg will meet personally with Jabbar to hand over the weapons!"

"Finally, we have a target window—that is, if Al can tell us where the exchange will take place," his partner said.

"We cannot report this up the line," he concluded. "If we do and these events don't materialize, it will be the final straw for the agencies. They will disperse our team and our best chance to get Heilberg and Jabbar will be lost."

"John, you don't dare take a team into Iran without sanction," she cried. "If something went wrong, you would be disavowed."

"As soon as we have actual coordinates, I will contact Kinsdale for immediate approval to take in the strike team," he assured her.

Melina reached for her husband's hand and said, "When this is over and Heilberg is no longer a threat, I am going to take a leave of absence from Alliance Base. I hope you are prepared to make lots of trips to Paris."

"Believe me, my darling, I can hardly wait," he sighed while pulling her into his arms.

Within 72 hours, a rotating surveillance schedule was established for the 12 members of the team. They were divided into three groups of four members, each standing an eight-hour shift. Melina stood watch with the morning group; she and John supervised the afternoon team together; and John stayed on to keep vigil with the overnight group.

This routine continued for four days with no action, and the agents were growing weary from boredom and the odd sleeping patterns. Despite repeated messages placed in the secret mail box in Tehran, there was no further communication from Al.

The Danish embassy was enclosed in a walled enclave along with all of the other foreign consulates represented in Islamabad. A vehicle carrying a bomb would be unlikely to get past the security post that guarded the main entrance to the community. Unfortunately, the Danish facility was set closest to the protective wall, and a large bomb detonated outside the fence could cause major damage to the building. Likewise, if an armed terrorist attack occurred, it would be fairly simple to breach the wall to get to the embassy.

The surveillance teams were camouflaged and placed in strategic positions along a tree-lined street outside the tall barrier. Traffic on the road was minimal; no more than a dozen cars typically used the passageway each day.

All of that changed on the afternoon of the fifth day. John was situated at one end of the block, and Melina was at the other end with three of the four team members. It was John who was the first to see an older model, orange Toyota roll onto the street just beyond Melina's vision. He called her on the walkie-talkie to alert her, and that is when he realized Ali was in the car. He was struggling with the driver for control of the vehicle, and suddenly, the passenger door flew open and his friend fell out into the pavement.

Immediately, Melina and the armed agents rushed toward the Toyota with their guns blazing. John screamed into his communicator for her to stop, but his words fell on deaf ears. He leaped from his hiding spot and ran into the street in the direction of the approaching car.

There was a tremendous explosion accompanied by a blinding light, and the concussive force lifted John off of his feet and thrust him backward. He had a momentary sensation of flying before everything went black.

Chapter 6

He sensed that people were talking, and there were alterations in light intensity long before he attempted to open his eyes. When he finally marshaled the strength to try, his eyelids seemed to weigh ten pounds each. With great difficulty, he focused his vision and saw that everything was white. He was thirstier than he had ever been in his life, and he tried to plead for a drink of water. What came out sounded more like the mating call of a bullfrog than any human voice.

"Holy smokes! He's awake," someone cried. "Go get the nurse."

There was a brief scramble as a person left the room. John felt exhausted, and he closed his eyes for a moment. When he opened them again, there was a man sitting at his bedside.

"I thought you might be ready to wake up again," the voice said. "Here, take a sip of water before you try to speak."

A drinking straw was placed to John's lips, and he pulled cool liquid into his parched mouth. It was refreshing, but he needed to close his eyes. He felt a hand nudge his shoulder gently.

"Come on, John. Stay with me," the man's voice coaxed. "You have slept long enough, buddy."

He focused his eyes on the face hovering close by and rasped, "Adrian Griffith? Is that you?"

"It's me, all right. Welcome back, pal."

"'Where am I?" he asked. "How long have I been here?"

"You are at the PIMS hospital; you've been out for two weeks," Griffith said as he twisted to look over his shoulder. "Oops! Here they come. The staff is going to toss me out of here, but I promise to be back as soon as I can."

True to his prediction, Griffith was ushered out of the room while a gaggle of doctors and nurses poked and prodded the patient for several minutes. John tolerated this activity as though he had no will of his own. When he was prompted with a question, he replied mostly in one word answers. At last, a physician, who was evidently the senior member of the medical team, requested that everyone withdraw. When he was alone with the patient, he stepped to the bedside and introduced himself.

"Mr. Pilgrim, my name is Dr. Salim Ghazini and I am the chief neurologist for the hospital," he said in near perfect English. "I am sure you have many questions, and I will try to answer them as best I can. However, I want to caution you to remain calm and not overtax yourself. Your body and mind have been through a difficult trauma, and you need time to rest and adjust."

"I was told that I have been here for two weeks; how much damage did I endure?"

"You were unconscious when you arrived here, and you remained in a persistent coma for 14 days," the doctor said. "Your left shoulder was dislocated and you had several deep, soft tissue hematomas. The most severe injury was caused by a metal shard that pierced your upper abdomen. In surgery we had to remove your spleen and about 10 centimeters of your small intestine. The operation was successful, and you should make a complete recovery."

"Complete recovery? You must be joking, doctor!" John groaned in misery. "What about my team?

Did any of them survive? There was a woman—where is she?"

"I am terribly sorry, but you were the only survivor," Dr. Ghazini answered. He checked a page on the clip board he was carrying. "Ah, yes, there was a Melina Chartres. Her body was cremated and the ashes were transported to Paris."

A withering cry erupted from John's throat and he wept uncontrollably. "No, it's not possible," he pleaded between racking sobs.

The physician was shocked by his patient's reaction. "Please calm yourself, Mr. Pilgrim. I am so sorry for your loss, but you cannot afford to become so agitated. Because of your coma, I dare not give you any medication to sedate you."

"Get the hell out of here and leave me alone!" John croaked. "Just go away."

"I will give you a chance to grieve and I will return tomorrow." Ghazini blurted before hurrying away.

John knew the true meaning of a breaking heart, for his sorrow had fractured him to the depths of his soul. He was so full of grief for his lost wife and unborn child that he had no room to mourn for his dead comrades. He wept uncontrollably, harder than ever in his life. His head pounded and his chest ached as though it might burst. He welcomed the pain; he embraced it and begged for it to take his life. If he died, surely he could rejoin his loved ones. In a frenzy, he grasped the IV lines and the leads to the coronary monitor and ripped them from his body.

Within moments, two nurses—one female and the other a male—were in his room. When they tried to restrain their rampaging patient, he thrashed about violently and threw a weak, ineffective punch at the male attendant.

"Get me a sedative in a hypo," the woman directed. "We must get this man some relief."

"The attending physician said he was not to be sedated," her colleague warned. "He doesn't want him to slip back into a coma."

"This man's blood pressure and heart rate are through the roof," she said. "He is going to have a stroke or cardiac arrest if we don't do something. Get me the damn meds!"

The male nurse scurried off and returned quickly with a loaded syringe and handed it to her. The patient was too agitated to administer the sedative in a vein, so she jabbed the needle into his shoulder muscle. It took longer than by IV, but within ten minutes John had calmed down and shortly afterward drifted off to sleep.

When he awoke again, Adrian Griffith was back in the room. The visitor put down the paperback novel he was reading and came over to the bed.

"You have had a nice nap," Griffith said. "I talked to you two days ago."

"What are you doing here?" John wheezed as he turned his face away. "I'm tired, Adrian. I just want to sleep."

"You can't do that, pal. You have checked out long enough," Griffith countered gently. "It is time to rejoin the living."

"I have no reason to live, so why don't you just get out of here," John whispered.

"That is not going to happen either. She would want you to live and so do I."

"What are you talking about?" John demanded with his face still averted.

"I am talking about Melina, of course. Come on, John; I was on your surveillance team. Everybody knew there was something going on between you two. Don't you think she would want you to live?"

Hot tears welled up and he fought to hold them back. He murmured, "When I see her, perhaps she will tell me."

"You still have work to do, John. If you give up, her killers will probably get away with it."

"Why do you care?" This time he looked at Griffith.

"Because you are worth the effort. I am going to be here every day for as long as I can. I will help you get through this whether you want me to or not."

"Don't waste your time."

"Hey, it is my time to waste—at least until Kinsdale forces me to leave. So, let me give you an update of events while you were resting. Our best intelligence is that Heilberg made good on his delivery of weapons to Jabbar's terrorist group. We assume the goods are squirreled away in various warehouses in and around Tehran. It was Heilberg, by the way, who provided the explosives to create the god-awful, big bomb that blew up our team. He and Jabbar are both hiding in parts unknown, but their mujahidin have made incursions into Afghanistan and have taken over some of the border towns already."

"What is Kinsdale doing about it?" John asked.

"Absolutely nothing," Griffith replied. "The Afghan security force is being deployed to oppose the insurgents, and the Company has pulled our agents off of the mission. There will be no covert operation to go after Heilberg and Jabbar unless they can be captured or killed outside the borders of Iran."

"Maybe, I will stick around after all, so I can find the people who did this myself," John said with grim conviction.

"If revenge is the juice that will get you going, then I'm all for it," Griffith concurred "When do we get started?"

Chapter 7

It had been two weeks since John had been discharged from the Pakistan Institute of Medical Sciences, or PIMS as it was generally called, and Griffith was taking him to a follow-up visit and his last physical therapy session at the hospital. This was also going to be Griffith's last week in Pakistan, because he was being recalled to Langley for a stateside assignment.

"I feel bad about leaving you so soon, but I must admit I miss my wife and kids terribly," he said as he pushed John's wheelchair toward Neurology. The patient was perfectly capable of walking, but hospital policy dictated otherwise. "I still think you should come back with me."

"I would enjoy meeting Marta and your son and daughter, but it will have to wait for a later time," John said. "I'm not ready to leave Pakistan yet."

"Yes, well, we need to have more discussion about that, mister."

They arrived at Dr. Ghazini's office, who had recovered enough from his lapse in bedside manner to continue as John's physician. Griffith remained in the waiting area with the wheelchair when the nurse ushered John into the treatment room. He sat down next to the examination table and noticed that several films were mounted on the light board. The details were not visible because the backlight was turned off. After a few moments, the neurologist entered the room and greeted him.

"You are looking quite well. I believe you have gained back some of the weight you lost following surgery," Ghazini observed. He flipped on the light board and used his pen as a pointer to indicate an area on one of the films. "There is the faintest hint of shadow in this lower section of the brain, which is unusual. I would have expected the concussion you endured would be reflected by changes in this upper area called the cerebellum."

"Is that a problem I need to be concerned with," John asked.

"Not necessarily. Your EEG readings of brain activity look normal. I recommend you schedule an MRI annually for at least the next three years. If any changes occur in brain histology, they would be identified early, but for the present, I think you can forego further visits for the next three months. Do you have any questions for me, Mr. Pilgrim?"

"No, but thanks for your care, Doctor," John said as he rose to shake hands. "Goodbye."

"Good luck to you, Mr. Pilgrim," Ghazini reciprocated, and he held open the door.

The physical therapy session consisted of walking for 20 minutes on a treadmill with electronic sensors attached to his chest and major muscle points. When his treatment was finished, the physical therapist, who spoke very little English, conversed with John in Urdu.

"You must continue your stretching exercises and walking," she counseled. "Be cautious to not overextend your left shoulder. It will take several months for muscles and ligaments to fully heal from the dislocation."

As they exited the department, Griffith popped open the wheelchair.

"Leave that here for someone who needs it," John commanded. "We are through with this place."

"Okay, John, that's the spirit!" Griffith crowed, as he shoved the chair against a wall.

On the drive back to the CIA facility where they had temporary quarters, Griffith broached the subject of what John intended to do once he was alone in Islamabad.

"You aren't still toying with the notion of going after Heilberg and Jabbar by yourself, are you?" he asked. "Because if you are, I want to be the first to tell you it's an insane idea."

"I agree it is a crazy fantasy," John replied. "Any man who would attempt such a thing would be someone who had nothing to lose."

"That is correct—he would be alone in a hostile land without help or supplies, and if he was captured, his own country would deny any connection to him. The poor stiff would either suffer a short but miserable existence in an Iranian prison or be publicly humiliated and beheaded."

"You have made your point, Adrian. Don't worry about me," John said. "Can we change the subject, please?"

"Sure, but there is something I want to give you," Griffith said as he reached into his coat pocket. He pulled out a slip of paper and handed it over without taking his eyes off of the traffic. "That is the number of a clean, unlisted phone that I happen to have in my possession. If you ever need help, give me a call."

John accepted the gift and asked, "Why have you taken such an interest in my welfare, Adrian? You were a member of my team, but we really did not know too much about each other. Is it some kind of survivor guilt? Do you feel a displaced responsibility for me because you were lucky enough to be on the third shift when the bomb went off?"

"No, it is nothing like that. The first time I met you I sized you up as one of the good guys," Griffith answered. "It's hard to explain, but I have this feeling that you have important work to do, and I am supposed to help you."

"If you are talking about God, He and I are not on speaking terms right now."

"Honestly, pal, that is between you and Him. I'm just trying to do my part."

Three days later, Griffith was on a plane headed for Washington, DC, and John was left to plan his visit to Tehran. Sitting alone in the small room, the desolate sense of loss began to creep over him again, and he knew he had to put a stop to it. If he surrendered to his grief, he would be unable to function. Rage and a desire for vengeance were needed to fuel his resolve. He turned his thoughts to Dieter Heilberg and Jabbar, and his mind burned with hatred for the murderers of his wife and child.

He stepped into the bathroom and splashed water on his face. He gazed at his image in the mirror above the basin. Although he had not shaved his face since his discharge from the hospital, he was struck again by how ordinary he appeared. He longed to return to the dark and ruthless persona of Charles Aragon. Standing there, he decided he would regrow his moustache and color his hair in a shade that was almost black. He would resurrect the deadly Aragon for the mission he hoped to carry out.

During the following three weeks, John used his rage as the driving force for physical exercise. He spent hours in the basement firing range reaffirming his skill with his handgun. On two occasions when his section chief, Mike Kinsdale, directed him to come back to the States, John convinced him that he required more space to heal before traveling. Time was running out, and John knew he would need to disappear or be forced to return to Langley, Virginia.

The day after his second conversation with his CIA supervisor John received a packet that confirmed the decision for him.

"This was delivered by hand for you at the security desk," the duty officer said, as he tossed a brown envelope onto John's cot. "The scanner showed it was nothing but paper."

He thanked the agent and waited for him to leave before opening the package. What fell out was infuriating. It was an eight by ten glossy photograph of the bomb site at the Danish embassy. The barrier fence was obliterated and the front of the embassy showed considerable blast damage. The ruined street was littered with fragments of the Toyota that delivered the explosive device. On the back of the photo there was a handwritten note addressed to John from Heilberg.

"I am glad you survived the detonation. It gives me immense pleasure to know you are suffering every day over the death of your comrades and especially that bitch, Melina. Just imagine the exquisite pain she endured when the bomb exploded!

"I will end your suffering soon enough, and I will make certain you know that your death is by my hand."

The message was signed simply as "D.H."

John folded the photo four times and tucked it into his wallet. That very afternoon he visited a local bank in which the Company maintained a numbered safe deposit box. He withdrew substantial sums of money—some in Euros, some in Iraqi dinars, but most in Iranian rials. He also pulled two passports from the box; one was French in the name of Charles Aragon and the other was Iraqi in the name of Abdullah Malik.

After he left the bank, he went shopping for clothes in a nearby marketplace. He rummaged through the second-hand stores until he found three outfits in his size. With his errands complete, he returned to the CIA facility to pack his knapsack. He placed all of his personal belongings, including his pistol and his Bible, in a sealed box inside a locker, and dressed himself as a local.

Shortly after dark, John walked out of the building and caught a taxi to a truck stop at the edge of the city. He hung around and chatted up the drivers until he found one headed for the narrow stretch of land where Pakistan, Afghanistan, and Iran converge. For the price of a pack of cigarettes and a promise to pay for meals, he caught a ride to the border.

He was committed now with no thought of turning back. He would enter Iran unarmed and alone to make his way to Tehran. Somehow, he would find Heilberg and deal with him. If he was successful, he would then focus his efforts on locating Jabbar. He would take every precaution to protect his own life until he completed his mission, but in his heart, he held little hope of ever returning from Iran.

Chapter 8

The driver's name was Galbadeen, and his destination was a primitive and lawless town called Zaranj that sits in the desert of Afghanistan a few miles from the Iranian border. It was a smuggler's paradise, and one of the principal commodities was an endless flood of immigrants hoping to find work in Tehran and the other larger cities of Iran. A man desperate enough to seek employment in this way was risking his very life. Within the space of a hundred miles, three countries abutted each other to form what has been called "the scariest little corner of the world."

John thanked his travel companion for the ride when the trip terminated at the local hospital in Zaranj. At a small general store, he purchased a couple of bottles of water and some strips of dried beef that he buried in his backpack. He walked the remaining few miles on foot to a desolate spot named Ganj where more than a hundred men squatted in the dust to pay for a ride across the border. Each time an empty truck appeared dozens of eager customers would rush to purchase a seat as human cargo. When no one else could climb aboard, the loaded-down vehicle would pull slowly away, and the hapless men left behind would return to their places in the dust.

John was careful not to offer too much to buy a place on the first few trucks that pulled through. In this dangerous place, a vagrant with extra money could get his throat cut. After a few hours, he caught a break on a flatbed truck with wooden slats for sides. He settled in as best he could for the 26-hour ride to Tehran.

He was exhausted from the earlier journey and the tedious wait in Ganj, and he dozed off despite the fact that he was jammed shoulder to shoulder with almost two dozen other immigrants. John awoke with a start when he felt something moving in his knapsack. He grabbed his neighbor's hand and jerked it out of the bag.

"Get away from me, you stupid thief!" he growled in Urdu. "If you come near me again, I will break all of the fingers of your right hand. I promise you will be unable to work for a month!"

The ragged vagabond pushed away, and with difficulty, threaded his way to the opposite end of the truck. John glared at the men nearest to him, and they all shrank back apprehensively. No one dared bother him for the remainder of the journey.

The truck driver unloaded his customers in one of the worst parts of the city. Several of the men would doubtlessly be assaulted and robbed of their meager possessions. One or two of them would never see another sunrise. For John's purposes, however, the area was perfect to his needs. In a back alley transaction, he purchased a .45 caliber handgun in fairly good shape. He also paid for an extra magazine of bullets.

A few doorways from the gun buy, he took a room in a seedy hotel. He locked the door and wedged a chair under the knob for extra security. It was late in the afternoon, and John decided he would wait until morning before he began his search. Being out on the streets at night was not an option.

He knew of two agents in Tehran that had broken off contact with the Company. When the CIA stopped providing support and funding, it was inevitable the informants would become silent. John hoped they were still alive and residing at their last known addresses. They were his only chance at connecting with the terrorist underground. He did not know if Heilberg was actually in the city, but he was certain either of the two former operatives would be better informed.

His thoughts turned to Ali and the indelible image of him struggling with the suicide bomber a moment before the car exploded. He missed his friend, and he desperately needed his help. The vision of Melina in her wedding dress joyfully hugging Ali slammed into his mind like a hammer. The pain it caused in his chest was unbearable. He reached into his wallet and found the brutal message from Heilberg and read it again. Fury replaced sorrow, and he vowed again to make the terrorist pay for his crimes.

Early the next morning, John dressed in the best of the three outfits he had purchased in Islamabad. With his new look of dark hair and moustache, he could easily pass for an Iranian citizen. He hid the gun beneath his tunic, collected his backpack, and strode out into the street. The prospects of finding a cab were unlikely, so he started walking toward the center of town. Ten blocks later, he was able to hail a taxi.

He gave the cabbie an address from memory, and it was fortunate the man spoke Urdu. John knew only a few phrases in Farsi. He introduced himself as Abdullah and the driver said his name was Navand. They negotiated for a bit over price; the destination was outside the city which meant John would probably be the only fare for the day. It took more than two hours to get to the village of Behan. It was little more than a wide spot in the road, but it had a gas station.

The mechanic on duty was a grizzled Kurdish man named Farhad Mazdani, and in the past he had been a steady source of information about the undercurrent of dissidents opposing the Ayatollahs. John remembered that he had his finger on the pulse of jihadist activities as well. He sent Navand to lunch at the only eatery in the town while he visited with Mazdani.

"How dare you show up here unannounced!" the mechanic shouted as soon as the driver was out of earshot. "You will get me and my family killed, you ignorant American!"

"I'm sorry. Tell me what I want to know and I will leave immediately," John said. "I am trying to find an arms dealer named Dieter Heilberg and a mullah named Abd al Jabbar bin Qadim al Islam."

"I never heard of them," Mazdani said as he began to clean grease off of his tools.

"Please don't lie to me, Fahrad, if you want me to go away," John scolded. "The last thing I want to do is put your family in jeopardy. By the way, are you still avoiding discovery by the Revolutionary Guard with your medical supply smuggling?"

"You CIA people are all alike. You start with the implied threats and move on to outright blackmail when you do not get what you want."

John ignored the barb. "Tell me what you know about these two men."

"I know very little. Both of them move around constantly to avoid being targeted. I believe they are in Tehran, but I do not know where. The best I can do is tell you where one of Heilberg's top thugs is staying."

"That is a start," John said. "Perhaps, he will be guide me to his boss."

"If I am lucky, perhaps he will cut your infidel throat instead," Mazdani muttered, but he scribbled down a name and address on a scrap of brown paper.

John accepted the note and thanked the informant, although the man had already turned his back on him. He walked across the narrow, pock-marked highway to the restaurant and found Navand. The cabbie was dawdling over an illegal glass of beer and flirting with the shopworn waitress. On the long ride back to the city, John pondered over the address the mechanic had given him. He recognized the location as a major boulevard in the downtown area, but he was unfamiliar with the exact spot.

He was surprised when the taxi pulled to a stop in front of the Mashad Hotel, a comfortable, mid-range lodge frequented by tourists and locals alike. If the man he was looking for was residing in the hotel, it was going to be extremely difficult to get to him without being noticed. He told the driver to take him two blocks farther down the street. John tipped Navand an extra million rials and told him to forget that they had ever met.

He got out of the cab and went shopping in the row of stores along the avenue. He bought himself a couple of high-end, off the rack suits and dressed in one of them before leaving the shop. A couple of doors down, he found shoes and a handsome leather suitcase to replace his knapsack.

Properly attired, John strolled into the Mashad Hotel, approached the front desk, and asked for the manager. The clerk left and a few moments later a thin, elderly man with a hawkish face came to the counter. He sized John up with a shrewd eye.

"How can I help you, sir?" the manager asked in Farsi.

John placed a passport on the marble top with the corner of a five-million rial note protruding from it. He answered in his best Arabic, "I do not have a reservation, but I need your finest room for a week. My name is Charles Aragon."

Chapter 9

The hotel manager was accommodating, but as he handed his guest a key card, he remarked, "I will expect to see your passport again when you check out, Mr. Aragon."

John knew the old crook was expecting another bribe at the conclusion of his stay, but it was worth it to have the hotelier on his side. A young bellhop hurried up to assist, and he handed the lad his key card and the brand new suitcase. The room was on the third floor, and the bellhop opened the door onto a spacious suite. The young man turned on the lights and adjusted the air conditioning before he looked expectantly at his guest. John tipped him 150,000 rials—equal to about five dollars—and the bellhop acted as though it was his birthday.

John pulled out the slip of paper that Mazdani had given him and asked the bellhop, "Do you know if Mr. Vahid Gol is staying here in the hotel?"

The boy looked frightened, but he answered honestly, "Yes, sir, he has a suite like yours on the fourth floor. Number 406."

"He is a former business acquaintance and I want to surprise him," John lied. "Please don't mention to anyone that I asked about him."

The bellman seemed relieved and he replied, "I will not say anything, sir. Please don't tell anyone that I gave you Mr.Gol's room number."

John assured him he would keep his confidence, and the young man backed his way hastily out of the room. There was little doubt the kid was scared to death of the resident in room 406. The mere fact that

Gol was living in a suite in the hotel was evidence he was high up in Dieter Heilberg's chain of command. It was also a sign he felt safe and insulated here in Tehran, and that made him vulnerable.

For the next two days, John followed his quarry. He discovered immediately there were two other thugs staying in the suite with Gol. The trio spent their time eating in restaurants along the boulevard in the daytime and taking women to the room at night. This was brazen behavior to indulge in right in the heart of fundamental Islam. Clearly, Heilberg was well-connected and his people were receiving a pass from the Revolutionary Guard.

It was also clear the three henchmen were not going to lead him to their boss. John's situation was precarious; it was just a matter of time before he would become the object of unwanted attention. He needed to take a more direct approach to extract information from Gol, but he could not risk an interrogation in the hotel.

An opportunity presented itself on the morning of the third day. Instead of their usual day of sloth, the group had a car brought around to the front of the hotel. John had to scramble to grab a taxi, and he directed the driver to follow the receding sedan. The journey ended in a warehousing district well south of the downtown area. John had no choice but to abandon the cab and work his way as close as practical to the building in which Gol and his companions had disappeared.

About 20 minutes later, they reappeared with each man carrying a heavy box—two long ones and one square one—that they loaded into the trunk of the car. Gol went back to lock the door of the warehouse before they drove away. John waited for a few minutes to insure no other activity would occur. He crossed the open area of the parking lot to the building and tried all of the doors. He had no luck getting in until he found a small window to a toilet that was cracked open slightly. He looked around until he found a length of rebar that had been flattened on one end and used it as a crowbar to jimmy open the sash.

He struggled to get through the small opening, and afterwards, he walked out into the darkened storage bay. He could tell that the place was filled with lots of amorphous shapes, and he felt his way along the perimeter until he came upon a light switch. He leaned against the wall in surprise when he could see he had discovered a huge stockpile of the weaponry Heilberg had procured for Jabbar.

Boxes were stacked high on pallets containing hundreds of Russian Kalashnikov AK-12 rifles. There were thousands of rounds of 7.62 mm ammo, also of Russian origin. As he moved throughout the huge room, he found four armored personnel carriers, mortars with shells, and shoulder-launched missiles. Almost all of the weapons were from Russia. In one area, he found a cache of riot control devices, including tear gas canisters, Tasers, and flash bombs.

John went into a small office that was sparsely furnished, but it included a couple of four-drawer file cabinets. He went through the files in hopes of finding an address or a map to show where Heilberg and Jabbar were hiding. He did not find what he was looking for, but he opened a folder that caused him to sit down at the desk in shock.

The file contained a front and back photocopy of a CIA check for over five million dollars made payable to the Pakistan defense department. The funds had been deposited into an account in a bank in Burma. A copy of a bank statement was also in the folder. The account number matched the endorsement on the back of the check, but the account holder was not the Pakistan defense department. It was a company that translated as Mid-Asia Investment Holdings. It was obviously a front for one Heilberg's various sources of money. All of this was of keen interest to John, but the one item that had him shaking his head was the name of the signer on the check. In a scrawl John recognized right away was the signature of Mike Kinsdale.

He pocketed the documents before returning the file folder to the cabinet just as he found it.

The contents of the warehouse were not all of the vast arms purchase Heilberg had acquired, but they were a significant portion. John knew he could not allow Jabbar's terrorist group to keep the armaments. The cache must be destroyed.

He went searching for the components he needed, and while he was occupied, a plan also formed in his mind that would allow him to lure Vahid Gol and the other two thugs away from the hotel. John was confident Gol would reveal everything he knew under the interrogation session John intended to host.

Chapter 10

It was an irksome challenge to get back to the Mashad Hotel dressed in a rumpled suit with no vehicle at his disposal. After walking for more than two miles, John caught a break with a farmer driving an ancient truck filled with oranges. The aged peasant took pity on him and gave him a ride into town. John had with him a long, slender package wrapped in canvas and tied up with string. The old man eyed the familiar looking item his rider was carrying, but he was cautious enough to not ask questions.

The farmer detoured out of his way to drop off John around the corner from the hotel front entrance. The passenger slipped a one million rial note into the driver's hand, and the old gentleman tried vigorously to refuse it. Finally, when John insisted, he accepted the gift with profound gratitude. He had just doubled his daily profit for selling a truckload of fruit.

John preferred to avoid the spectacle of strolling through the main lobby in a soiled and wrinkled suit while toting a wrapped package that looked suspiciously like a rifle. He went around to the rear of the hotel and found the service entrance. He flashed his key card at a cook as he hurried through the kitchen to the employee's elevator. He got off at the third floor and rushed into his suite, doing his best to shield his package from the view of the video cameras placed at either end of the hallway.

He took a shower and dressed in clean clothes before sitting down to consider what to do next. John's plan was compromised by the security video located on every floor. An idea came into his head, and he went to the closet to pull his old knapsack from the bottom of his new suitcase. He unwrapped the package he had brought from the warehouse to reveal one of the Russian-made military rifles. He broke the weapon down into two pieces and secured them in the bag. With the knapsack in hand, it was time to go shopping again.

He left the hotel to browse the clothing stores once more. In a woman's shop, he found a traditional black burka, complete with the veil. He paid for the outfit and asked to use the dressing room. John covered himself completely with the burka and veil and then removed the rifle from the backpack. He assembled the weapon and hid it effectively within the folds of the dress. He left the empty satchel and strolled out of the store before anyone noticed him. Within minutes, he had returned to the Mashad.

With his head bowed, he moved across the lobby waiting area directly to the elevators. He had the lift all to himself, and he pressed the button for the fourth floor. Keeping his head lowered as before, John walked down the hallway to room 406. He removed the AK-12 from the cloth of the dress and leaned the weapon at an angle against the door. He returned at once to the elevator and went back to the first floor to exit the hotel. He strolled a block away from the lodging, ducked down an alley, and shed the smothering garment. He threw the burka in a large trashcan and retraced his path to the Mashad, but he did not go inside.

Instead, he hailed one of the cabs stationed near the entrance and directed the driver to take him back to the warehouse district. John knew he had to have the rest of his plan in place before Heilberg's men returned to their suite and discovered the rifle.

Getting into the building that contained the weapons was much easier this time, because John had left the door unlocked. He went straight to the crowd control devices and obtained what he needed. He constructed a relay of tear gas and flash grenades in a large ring near the entrance. He attached a tiny, remote-controlled detonator to the network of canisters and put the controller in his pocket. He searched through boxes until he found a couple of Taser guns and a gas mask that he hooked to his belt. Finally, he took another AK-12 rifle with extra magazines of ammo and went outside to find the best sniper location from which to observe the doorway into the warehouse.

He settled for a second-floor room in the building directly across the pavement from the weapons storage. There was a window facing the warehouse entrance, and next to the window was a door that opened onto a fire escape stairway. John broke through a window on the first floor to gain access and went upstairs to set up and wait for Heilberg's crew to arrive.

About two hours later, a black sedan and a gunmetal gray van roared up and came to a screeching halt at the warehouse. Gol and his two henchmen got out of the sedan with handguns drawn, and four men in military fatigues boiled out of the van, each with a rifle. One of Gol's lieutenants sidled up to the door to unlock it, and when he found it to be open, he signaled frantically to his boss.

Gol ordered the soldiers to enter the building, and he followed them along with his other companion. The thug who had tried the door was left outside to keep watch. John counted to five and pressed the remote. There was a tremendous noise and a cloud of smoke and fumes billowed out of the door opening. John fired a single bullet at the guard, and he dropped like a stone. He rushed out of the room and down the fire escape to sprint across the blacktop. He flattened himself against the wall of the warehouse and pulled on the gas mask.

He had descended now into that dark place of combat where there is no compassion, no mercy, and only the call of killing and death is heeded.

Crouching low to the ground, John somersaulted into the darkened storage bay. Two bullets whizzed close by as he was silhouetted momentarily in the light of the doorway. He scuttled forward in the inky mist to hone in on the coughing and gagging sounds coming from the assault team. From his position, he could have easily cut down the entire group, but he needed Gol and his roommate alive. He squatted in the dark and waited.

Two of the foot soldiers were the first to break for the outside, and John shot them both just as they cleared the doorway. Immediately, he rolled hard to his left and barely avoided a spray of bullets directed at his previous spot. Gol and his people were incapacitated but still shrewd enough to aim at the muzzle flash from John's rifle.

They were not likely to repeat the mistake of their dead comrades, and that presented a difficult problem for John. He still had four armed men to deal with even though he could hear their muffled choking noises. He decided to go for broke, and he belly crawled back toward the doorway. He reached up and felt for the light switch. When he found it, he turned and sat up with his back against the wall. He pulled the two Taser guns from his belt and placed one on the floor to his left side and the other to his right. He held the AK-12 steady with one hand, reached above his head with the other, and flipped on the lights.

The sudden illumination added to the confusion of his opponents, and John was able to get off a couple of shots. The rounds found their mark in the two remaining soldiers, but Gol and his lieutenant, still blinded and hacking from the tear gas, fired wildly in John's direction. One of the bullets grazed his shoulder, but he remained focused and grabbed the Tasers off the floor. He fired both at the same time; one projectile caught Gol's subordinate in the left thigh, and the other imbedded in Gol's right shoulder. Both men convulsed as 50,000 volts coursed through their bodies.

They collapsed onto the floor, twitching and incapacitated, and John looked at them with the same detachment one might feel toward a bug. He glanced at the shallow wound on his arm with the same cold disinterest. He did not feel fear, or relief, and certainly not remorse. He could feel only hate and a desire for retribution. It was his only purpose for moving forward.

Chapter 11

It took about fifteen minutes for the air handlers to clear the warehouse of tear gas. John used the time to securely bind Vihad Gol and his sidekick to a couple of chairs. There was a first aid kit in the office, and he used a compression bandage to dress his wound. Next, he dragged the three bodies that lay outside back into the building and moved the van to the rear of the warehouse. He had one last task to complete before he revived his two captives.

He went to the huge ammunition storage located in the middle of the warehouse and wired up a series of detonators that could be fired from a single remote control device. He also collected an additional transmitter and two more of the explosive caps. Blowing up the huge cache of armament would not only put a big dent in Jabbar's plans for terrorism it would also be sure to gain Heilberg's attention and hopefully draw him out.

He returned to his captives and placed the extra detonators and control device in his ammo canister. Once this task was finished, he was ready to interrogate the prisoners. John removed his gas mask and tentatively took a whiff. The air had been cleansed sufficiently, and he no longer needed protection. He found a small bucket and filled it with water from the washroom. He went back to where he had left the two men tied up.

Gol was moaning and semiconscious and John doused him with water. That got a reaction and started to bring him around. John flooded the other man as well, but he woke up retching and screaming. Both captives had raw, swollen eyes from the prolonged exposure to the tear gas. John slapped the underling hard with his open hand and that stopped the caterwauling.

"Who are you and what do you want?" Gol rasped in Arabic, blinking his eyes painfully.

"I am the person that holds your life in his hands. What I want is very simple. Where is your boss? Tell me that and this will all be over."

"I don't know what you are talking about. I am a simple businessman, and I have no boss."

John withdrew the handgun he had purchased in the alley and used it for the first time to blow away the right kneecap of Gol's companion. The man shrieked in agony and terror. John allowed the bellowing to go on for a while, but then he grabbed the wounded man by the shirt front and shoved the pistol under his jaw.

"Shut your mouth or I will shut it permanently," he commanded.

The bleeding captive reduced the noise to labored gasps for air, and John returned his attention to Gol.

"Don't lie to me. Your name is Vihad Gol and you work for Dieter Heilberg. If you tell another lie, I will destroy both of your knees, and you will be never walk properly again."

"All right, you know who I work for, so you must also know that you are a dead man. Heilberg will find you and kill you. He will kill your family and all of your friends."

"He has already done that. I have nothing else to lose."

The prisoner's red and blotchy face contorted in fear. "You are Aragon, aren't you? Charles Aragon! Listen, I had nothing to do with what happened to your sister, or whatever she was to you."

"You have ten seconds to tell me where I can find Heilberg."

John pressed the muzzle of the gun against Gol's right knee, and the thug struggled desperately to get away.

"Time's up!"

"Wait! Wait, damn it, I don't know where he is!" Gol babbled. "All I do is standby for orders. He contacts me when he needs me. He is too paranoid to stay in one place. I swear I don't know where he is!"

"Heilberg's two wives and his children have disappeared from Egypt. Has he moved them here to Tehran?"

"I don't know. I'm just a foot soldier; he does not tell me such personal things."

"That is a lie!" John pressed the gun barrel against the man's right knee and pulled the trigger.

Gol screamed as the joint disintegrated, spraying bone and blood onto the captive next to him. The gunshot set the subordinate howling again, and both prisoners screamed and struggled violently against their bindings. John stood and watched this horror show for a few moments with merciless eyes. He stepped forward and shot Gol's underling in the forehead just between the eyes, and the man went limp instantly, slumping in the chair like a sack of potatoes. Wounded and suffering, Gol stopped bellowing and stared at his captor in shock and terror.

"You are insane! My friend knew as much as I do, and you killed him without asking a single question!"

"I do not have the time or patience for a long-term relationship," John said sardonically. "If you want to live through this experience, give me the address where Heilberg is keeping his family. Do it now!"

"They are hiding in a house at 9000 Babibandz Street," Gol babbled without hesitation. "The women and children are heavily protected by guards. You will never get to them."

"See. That wasn't so difficult, was it?" the devil standing before him said in a voice as cold as ice.

"Are you CIA?" Gol asked tentatively; when his captor did not answer, he said, "You *are* CIA! Why are you doing this? Have you been sent to erase the connection between Heilberg and your spy organization? Have we become an inconvenience to your government?"

"What are you chattering about?" John asked. "What does the CIA have to do with this?"

"You fool!" the suffering terrorist moaned through his pain. "This has been all for personal revenge. You don't even know that your own masters helped finance the weapons purchase for Imam Jabbar. They are more responsible for the deaths of your people than we are."

"You are lying!" John snarled, pointing the pistol directly at Gol's head.

Gol cringed in anticipation of receiving a bullet through the brain like his companion, but he blurted out, "No, I am not. Go into the office and open the locked drawer of the desk. There is a spare key taped to the underside of the chair. Inside, you will find a folder marked 'Accounting.' Look at the first page in the file!"

John stalked back to the office and did as Gol had directed. When he extracted the page, he saw it was a bank transfer authorization. It showed that fifty million dollars had been moved from an investment firm John recognized as a front organization for the Company. The funds were deposited into a numbered account in a Swiss bank. The name of the authorizing officer at the bottom of the slip sent a shaft of ice up John's spine.

He folded the page and slipped it into the same pants pocket where he had earlier secured the other documents. He returned to where he had left Gol tied up and sitting next to his friend's corpse. Without even taking notice of his hostage, John collected his knapsack, an assault rifle, and a canister of ammo that he had placed nearby. He walked toward the door to leave.

"Heilberg will destroy you," the suffering thug cried after him. "I hope you die slowly, begging for death."

John hesitated at the doorway, and without looking back, he said over his shoulder, "When I suggested you could live through this, I lied."

Filled with rage and renewed bravado, Gol yelled after the disappearing tormentor, "I am not afraid to die, kafir! I am mujahidin!" Only the echo of the empty warehouse answered him back.

Outside in the bright sunlight, John stowed the AR-12 and bullets in the trunk of the black sedan before sitting in the driver's seat. He pulled away quickly but slowed down just before leaving the warehousing complex. He pressed the button on the remote control device, and an enormous explosion occurred at the weapons storage building. As he drove away, the booming sounds of multiple detonations punctuated his departure while a horrendous fireball rose into the late afternoon sky.

Chapter 12

On the outskirts of Tehran, John stopped at a bazaar to purchase a black outfit suitable for night time surveillance. At a used clothing kiosk, he found a pullover and dungarees, as well as a black leather jacket in good condition. At another stand, he bought an older-model Pentax SLR digital camera with a telephoto lens for a good price. He ordered a rice and meat kabab at an outdoor food bar and washed it down with a bottle of lemonade before continuing his journey back to the city. Along a deserted stretch of road, he pulled over and changed his attire into the black clothing

Later, he refueled the car and bought a map of Tehran, and then he made his way to the location that Gol had yielded on Babibandz Street. It was two-story house with a high privacy wall around the back yard and an iron fence with a gate across the driveway in front. John drove by without stopping and noticed there were two guards stationed at the gate and another on the porch near the door.

He worked his way through the neighborhood until he found the street closest to the rear of the house. Fortunately, there was a three-story store for rent almost parallel to the residence of the Heilberg families. The building was empty with a small parking area in back. John made sure no one was watching before he used a fire escape alongside the house to climb to the top floor. There was a bit of acrobatics required when he balanced on the bannister to get a purchase on the edge of the flat roof. With both the camera and rifle slung across his body, John pulled himself up and over the ledge onto the roof. He grimaced from pain as he overextended his damaged shoulder.

For the next hour or so, he sprawled on his belly on the gravel surface and observed the activity in the back yard through the telephoto camera lens. Both of Heilberg's wives and all four of the children moved in and out of the house into the private yard. John took dozens of pictures of the group until twilight made it too gloomy for more photos. He got a couple of final shots through the light of the kitchen window of the two women working together preparing dinner, before packing up and cautiously crawling off of the roof.

John drove toward the Mashad Hotel but stopped first in the commercial district to find a business services store. He discovered one still open, and he used a color copier to access the memory card from his camera. He scrolled through the images on the small monitor until he found a half dozen pictures that clearly identified every member of Heilberg's family. He made printouts of his selection and placed the sheets in a mailing envelope before going to the counter to pay for the services. He scribbled Vihad Gol's name and room number on the envelope with instructions to hold the packet for Dieter Heilberg, and he signed it from simply "C.A."

Arriving at last at the hotel, he parked temporarily in the unloading area while he went in to the counter and handed the front desk clerk the envelope with a generous tip. The attendant had to bend the envelope into a semicircle to get it to fit in the cubbyhole for room 406. John hurried back to the car so he could return to the Heilberg family's safe house. He was careful to make sure he was not being followed, and he was relieved to find that no one had identified him in the lobby.

He found a spot a few blocks from 9000 Babibandz Street that allowed him to watch traffic heading in the direction of the house. John calculated it would not take long for Heilberg to be on full alert. By now, the news about the destroyed warehouse had surely reached him and attempts to contact Gol would be useless. As soon as Heilberg became aware of the photographs, he would be compelled to move his family.

There would be no way for John to approach his prey at this juncture. The weapons dealer and his family would be surrounded by a small army of armed guards. His best and probably only chance would be to follow the caravan to whatever alternate location Heilberg chose for the women and children. After they were installed in new quarters for a while without incident, the high level of security would very likely relax somewhat. John could only hope for a window during which Heilberg was still on site with his family but protection was reduced to a manageable level.

If possible, Heilberg should be kept alive long enough to tell John where the imam was hiding. After all, Jabbar was the one who had planned and ordered the attack on the Danish embassy that resulted in the death of his wife and child, as well as his dear friend, Ali, and four brave members of his team. If he did not get Jabbar, the job was only half finished.

About two hours had passed when a string of four SUV's rolled by John's observation point. His gut told him Heilberg was in one of those vehicles, and he struggled to refrain from chasing after them. He desperately wanted to pepper the vans with rifle bullets until he was certain his enemy was dead. He held on instead for 30 minutes before he tracked the SUV's. It was pitch black now, and the paved road soon turned to a dirt farm path. John pulled off of the road and killed the lights. He found an LED flashlight in the glove box and went to collect the assault rifle and ammo from the trunk. He used the sling to hoist the rifle onto his shoulder. He would make his way on foot the rest of the way.

It was amazing how quickly the busy, crowded city had dissipated into rugged terrain. He had walked for less than a mile when a narrow side road presented itself. John shined the flashlight on the intersection and he could see fresh tire impressions made by several vehicles. He was sure the caravan had taken the side road, so he turned off the beam and proceeded with caution.

There was a half-moon in the night sky that cast a dim silvery glow over the landscape. To be on the safe side, John elected to move quietly in the gully alongside the road rather than provide a silhouetted target in the diminished light. He prayed he would not step on an Oxus cobra or a Haly's pit viper in the dark, both of which were deadly night hunters native to Iran.

Soon up ahead, he could make out something hulking in the road. As he crept silently closer, he could tell that it was one of the SUV's from the convoy. A red glow brightened momentarily and then subsided. He realized it was one of the guards leaning against the back of the vehicle and smoking a cigarette. Another man was dozing in the passenger seat with his head resting on the open window frame. John squatted in place and waited.

He could not afford to use either his pistol or the rifle to take out the two sentinels. The sound of gunfire would surely alert the main party farther down the road. Besides, he needed the guards to be alive and waving in the event part of the security force rolled past after being reassigned to other duties. He remained in place as minutes ticked by and his ankles began to cramp. Finally, he saw lights illuminating the rough road as vehicles bumped and bounced toward the parked SUV. John hunkered down low to the ground to avoid the headlights as two vans roared by.

The security team had just been cut by half, and John hoped with morbid dread that Heilberg was not among the passengers in the departing motor cars. After a few minutes, the driver got out of the SUV and had another cigarette while his partner settled in to continue his nap. The guard crushed the butt of his smoke and walked in John's direction. He stopped not more than eight feet from where John was concealed and unzipped his trousers. The sound of liquid spattering on the weeds and the faint odor of ammonia drifted toward him as the man relieved himself.

When the driver finished and turned back toward the SUV, John knew he had to make his move. He stood and moved as quietly as possible onto the road and came up behind the unsuspecting guard. He reached around with his right hand and captured the man's windpipe in a vice-like grip. He gave him two vicious punches in the kidney with his left fist and the guard's legs buckled. John held onto him as he dropped to his knees and used the advantage to grasp the man's chin with one hand and a handful of hair on the back of his head with the other. He twisted upward with all of his might and snapped the sentry's neck.

The body twitched soundlessly for a moment and then lay still. The entire attack occurred in less than ten seconds. John pulled the guard off of the road and searched the body. He secured a combat knife from the man's belt, plus the keys to the vehicle, and a Zippo cigarette lighter in a pocket. John turned his attention to the man snoozing in the SUV.

The guard was snoring with his head on the window ledge. John made short work of him by slitting his throat with the blade he had taken off the sleeper's partner. He hauled the bloody corpse out of the vehicle and dumped it in the ditch.

John got into the SUV and drove it slowly with the lights off for about two miles. In the distance he could see part of a structure backlighted against the horizon. He parked the car, and with the rifle in one hand and the ammo box in the other, he traveled slowly and cautiously down the road. He came upon a farmhouse with a barn off to one side and some fenced pens. The remaining SUV was parked nearby, and two men were stationed on the lighted porch. He ducked into the scrub brush and observed the scene.

Within a few minutes, John had identified a third man in the dark near the barn and a fourth one standing in a grove of fruit trees to the right of the house. From his position, he could not determine if there was anyone on duty at the rear of the house, but he had to assume there was. In addition, there could be two or three more bodyguards inside the farmhouse to protect Heilberg and his family.

There was no way he could take out the guards one at a time and avoid being discovered and neutralized On the other hand, collecting all of these shooters in one place was going to be a real challenge. John knew he needed to create a diversion that was spectacular enough to cause all of them to rush to the same spot.

An idea came to him, but it meant getting to the SUV that was parked at the edge of the yard. The vehicle was sitting in the dark beyond the lights of the porch, but it would be difficult to approach it without being detected. John decided he had no other choice. He carefully opened the ammunition case and withdrew the two detonator bombs and the remote control device he had brought with him. He shed the rifle and began a slow, arduous belly crawl through low scrub brush toward the SUV.

He finally reached a point where he could avoid being seen by any of the sentries except the one standing post in the orchard. He caught a break a short while later when the guard strolled to the porch and spoke to the men stationed there. John scurried forward to the automobile and crawled under the rear bumper. He placed one magnetized bomb on the gas tank and the other as far forward as he could reach, activated them, and then hurried into the dark field before the guard returned. He carefully made his way back to the spot where he had left the weapon.

He laid the remote device on the ground beside him along with two extra magazines of bullets. He positioned the rifle and pressed the button. Instantly, one of the detonators blew up the gas tank and the other one sent the SUV in a somersault end over end. When it landed, it burst into flames. The explosion sent all four of the armed men rushing into the yard. The front door opened and another man stepped out, but he stayed on the porch.

John dispatched the one on the porch first and that triggered a hail of bullets from the others clustered near the burning wreck. He took aim as shells spattered around him like raindrops and dropped two of the shooters. It sent the remaining guards scrambling for cover, but it was too late for them. He caught one running for the door and the other just before he disappeared around the corner of the house.

Discarding the rifle, he pulled his handgun from his belt and sprinted for the porch. Before he could breach the doorway, a thug leaped into the opening and fired point blank at him. By all science, the bullet should have killed him, but the slug ripped cloth only.

John was unharmed. His opponent did not fare as well; he fell dead with two shots to the chest. He was in a blood fury now, and John leaped over the body looking for someone else to kill.

A closet door opened and a shrieking woman rushed out with a knife in her hands. John killed her without hesitation with a single shot to her forehead. There was someone else in the closet; a young boy who ran out and threw himself over the body of the woman.

"Mother!" the child cried out in Arabic.

John was still in the throes of bloodlust, and he hauled the boy up roughly and held him by the scruff of the neck while he cried and squirmed.

"Pilgrim! Don't hurt him; he is my son!" a voice called out in English.

John whirled in the direction of the sound, and there, brandishing a pistol with eyes filled with terror, was the man he came to kill—Dieter Heilberg!

Chapter 13

John pulled the youngster in front of him and pointed the pistol at his head. He growled at Heilberg, "Drop the gun or I will kill the boy."

There was a brief moment of hesitation, but Heilberg bent down without breaking eye contact and placed the weapon at his feet.

"Kick it over here," John commanded.

The arms dealer pushed the gun with his foot, and it slid to within inches of his captor.

"Stand here and don't you dare move." The child did as instructed while John reached for his wallet. He fumbled with one hand to extract the folded sheet that he shoved in the boy's fist. He said, "Give this to him."

The frightened youngster rushed to his father's arms and bawled, "He killed my mother!"

"Hush, Nabib," Heilberg urged. "Go in there to Fahima and help her with your brothers and sister." He took the paper from his son and gave him a push toward a closed door

John allowed the boy to go into the other room while the man unfolded the sheet and read it. Heilberg's face contorted in fear when he discovered it was the photograph and message he had sent to his enemy while he was in recovery.

"Don't hurt my family," the hostage pleaded.

"Why shouldn't I? You murdered mine," the man with the gun snarled.

"I don't know what you mean."

"Melina was my wife and she was carrying our unborn child."

"I had nothing to do with her death. Jabbar carried out the assault on the embassy. Jabbar is the person you want, not me."

"Tell me where he is and I will spare your children," John said in a voice thick with rage.

"He is not in Tehran anymore. He left two days ago for Afghanistan, but I have no idea where he is staying."

"Do not lie to me!" the crazed man bellowed.

"I am telling the truth; I swear it. There is a safe house in Kabul that he goes to sometimes. It is at number five Gamez Street; perhaps you will find him there. That is all I know."

"You are the one who provided Jabbar and his gang with the weapons and the means to carry out his bloody jihad," John seethed through clinched teeth. "The blood of my people, of my wife, of my child is on your hands."

At that moment, the door to the room containing the surviving wife and children opened and the boy name Nabib reappeared. John was distracted for only a second, but it gave Heilberg time enough to reach behind his back and pull another gun hidden in his belt. He whipped it forward, yet he was an eye blink too slow. John emptied half a clip into the man's chest. The impact slammed the arms dealer backward against the wall, and he slid down to a sitting position. Heilberg's dead eyes continued to burn a hole in John's own.

Nabib stood frozen in place. At last, he whispered, "You have killed my mother and my father. Are you going to kill me, too?"

"Not unless you force me to," John said to the child half his height. "I killed your father because he destroyed the people I loved. Your mother died because she gave me no choice. Someday, when you are older, you may wish to find me and exact revenge. If you do, I will understand how you feel, but I will resist being killed, and I am better at this than you will ever be. I hope you will make a different decision."

With that, he turned and walked out of the house, past the smoldering hulk of the SUV, through the yard littered with bodies of the men he had killed, and onto the darkened road. He trekked to the abandoned vehicle and drove it past the point where the two corpses lay discarded in the brush. Past the intersection where he had left the sedan, he changed cars with the intention of driving straight through to the border of Afghanistan.

Five minutes later, he began to shiver as though he was freezing despite the evening temperature being in the mid-seventies. His hands shook so violently, be could barely hold the car onto the road. Suddenly, his belly threatened to erupt, and he braked sharply. He threw open the door just before vomiting up everything his stomach could offer. He dry heaved several times before he could regain control.

John was gripped with sorrow so intense he could scarcely inhale. He had killed over a dozen men and a woman during the preceding twelve hours. He had avenged Melina's death and then some, but instead of feeling vindicated, he found himself wishing a bullet had put him out of his misery.

He changed his mind about Afghanistan; he simply could not continue. He pitched the handgun out of the window and drove directly to the Imam Khomeini International Airport in Tehran. He used his French passport to purchase a ticket on Iran Air for a direct flight to Paris.

As soon as the shops in the terminal opened, he bought a couple of changes of shirts and slacks and discarded the black clothing in the men's toilet. He found a quiet spot and sat down to wait until his flight was called. He desperately needed to find Melina's resting place. Perhaps then he could also find some peace.

Chapter 14

By the time the plane landed at Charles de Gaulle Airport, John had decided he had been under the radar long enough, and he dared not delay in checking with the office. He found a pay phone and used a personal credit card to place a call to his supervisor, Mike Kinsdale.

"Where are you, John?" Kinsdale asked cordially. "We have been concerned about you."

"I'm fine and I will be in Langley in a couple of days," John said, evading the question about his present location.

"I want you to meet with a couple of our people. I may have an assignment for you," Kinsdale said. "So, where did you say you are?"

Something did not feel right, and John responded, "A couple of days, Mike, and I will be in touch."

He hung up the phone and retrieved the cell number that Adrian Griffith had given him. He dialed the number. It was noon in Paris, which meant it was 6:00 am in Virginia. Griffith answered on the third ring.

"John! I'm glad to hear from you! Are you all right?" he exclaimed. "Kinsdale has a sanction out on you."

"I just spoke to him, and I gathered that something was off," John responded. "I am okay, Adrian, but what kind of sanction has he issued?"

"It is a 'pick up and detain' order, but the rider is 'with all due force.' The scuttlebutt is that you have gone rogue and entered Iran without authorization."

"I intend to show up in the next few days to clear this up," John deflected. "I will call you before I arrive to see what the temperature is."

"If you are coming in, don't fly into DC. He has agents watching all incoming flights."

"Thanks, Adrian. I want to walk in on my own and not in handcuffs."

"Be careful," Griffith said before he hung up.

John yearned to find Melina, but the information he had just received dictated that he take care of other business first. He caught a taxi and had the driver take him to the nearest postal service. He purchased several of two sizes of envelopes—one kind larger than the other—and found a private corner where he could write. He rented time on a copy machine to make multiple copies of the $5 million check and the $50 million bank transfer report from his suitcase and scribbled the same note along the bottom of each sheet.

The inscription was *Unauthorized, illegal funds transfer to terrorist organization.* He folded the sheets and placed them in the smaller envelopes. On the face of the envelopes he wrote his name and the instructions: *Open in event of my death, disappearance, or imprisonment.* He placed each sealed packet inside a larger envelope and addressed four of them to individuals he trusted with his life. He sent two others to himself at blind mail boxes he maintained in Orlando, Florida, and in Alexandria, Virginia. The seventh and last copy of each document was returned to a compartment in the suitcase along with the originals. He took his collection of letters to the counter and posted them.

He walked outside and looked for an opportunity to catch another taxi on the busy boulevard. There were plenty of cabs in the traffic, but they were not interested in picking up a curbside fare. A hotel was about a block away, and John strolled there to find an available driver. He walked down the line of waiting conveyances and flashed Eurodollars in his hand. One of the cabbies motioned to him, and John got into the back.

"Take me to St. Bernadette Catholic Church on the Rue du Mont Cenis," he told the driver in French, as he handed him a couple of bills.

The taxi man nodded and pulled out of line to negotiate his way into the traffic. He drove John across the city to the church without conversation. John paid his fare and got out near the front doors. He surveyed the venerable house of worship Melina had spoken of with such deep affection. There was a cemetery and mausoleum on the grounds, and John felt certain Melina's ashes would be interred there.

Overwhelming loneliness possessed him again, and he suddenly doubted his decision to come here. What was he hoping to find? The visit would surely not take away the pain. Was he looking for closure, or clarity, or redemption? He decided to try the massive doors and was surprised to find them unlocked. He stepped inside and walked into the sanctuary.

John was not Roman Catholic so he did not genuflect to the altar, but in reverence, he bowed slightly to the illuminated crucifix mounted on the wall. He took an aisle seat on one of the back pews. Sitting there in the silent, empty church, the full impact of his rampage in Iran rushed upon him. His thirst for vengeance had resulted in the death of a boy's mother along with the child's father and a dozen men. Yet, more than that, John had fully expected to die in Tehran in a kind of suicide by proxy.

He buried his face in his hands and tried to shut out the thoughts. He wanted to pray, but the words would not come. How could he expect God to listen to him after the things he had done?

John was startled out of his fugue when a voice asked in French, "Is there some way I can help you, my son?"

He looked up at a priest of about seventy years of age with snow white hair and slightly humped shoulders, a telltale sign of osteoporosis. He had a kind face that was pinched with worry.

"I apologize, Father. I'm not Catholic," John answered in English. "I just needed a few moments to prepare myself. I believe my wife's cremated remains may be preserved in your mausoleum."

"What is her name? Perhaps I can help you find her resting place," the priest offered, switching to English.

"I wouldn't want to take you away from your duties," John said, feeling awkward by the older man's concern. "Just direct me to where the most recent interments are located."

"I used to be the primary pastor here at St. Bernadette's, but now, I am practically in retirement. You would be doing me a favor if you allow me to assist you," the cleric explained, extending his hand. "My name is Father Pierre Sarkozy."

John stood up and shook hands. "Thank you; my name is John Pilgrim, and my wife's name is Melina Chartres."

"You are Melina's husband? I had no idea she was married."

"Did you know Melina, Father Sarkozy?"

"I baptized her as an infant, and she grew up as a member of our church community. She had not attended mass here for a while, but I would have thought she would inform me she was married."

"We were newlyweds of only about three months. I lost her before our lives together barely got started," John said miserably.

Tears began to spill from his eyes, and he turned away in embarrassment. He struggled to regain control, but the dam had broken. When he felt the priest put his hand on his shoulder, his resolve gave way completely. He sat down again and put his hands and forehead on the back of the pew in front of him as he succumbed to racking sobs.

Father Sarkozy tugged him by the arm and said, "Come with me, John. Let us walk out into the memorial garden and find your wife."

John allowed himself to be guided out of a side door near the chancel and into the afternoon sunshine. A light breeze carried a delicate scent of cherry blossoms. Nearby, a bird trilled a joyful song. The simple act of moving into a new venue helped him stem the tide of tears. He wiped his eyes with his hands and strolled silently beside the priest to the mausoleum.

"Here is our girl," Father Sarkozy said as he indicated a delicate blue and white ceramic urn placed in a small alcove of the wall. A modest plaque beneath the urn displayed simply her name and the dates of her birth and death. He continued, "Let's sit here and visit with Melina for a space."

He sat with his guest on a stone bench in front of the alcove and waited patiently until John was ready to talk.

"Who provided the vessel?" John asked, finally breaking the silence.

"We have a fund that is provided by our congregation to assist when family is unable to handle final expenses," Father Sarkozy said. "I selected the urn myself, but you could choose a different one, if you wish."

"No, you chose well. It suits her," John admitted. "I would like to make a donation to the fund, however. If there are any other expenses, I will also take care of them."

"I will arrange it. John. Can you tell me how Melina died?"

"I want to tell you everything, but I am restricted from sharing any details."

"You said you are not Catholic, but I am bound by oath to keep anything you tell me in confidence. Whatever you wish to say will remain private between you, me, and our Heavenly Father."

"I can tell you we were on a dangerous assignment together. Melina was murdered by a suicide bomber, but I was farther away and only injured. I was in a coma for several days, and when I revived, the decisions about Melina had already been made and carried out."

"I am so sorry. She was a lovely person with an unshakable moral code."

"That is not the whole story. Melina was pregnant with our child. The news was so recent we had not seen our first sonogram yet, so I did not get to even learn the gender of our baby."

"I had no idea," the old priest said, shaking his head with sadness. "Would you like for us to say a mass for your wife and child?"

"Yes, I would like that, and can we add a plaque to acknowledge our child and the date of death?"

"Yes, of course. I will take care of it. I will also pray for you, John."

"I don't think it will do any good, Father. I have done things—terrible, unforgiveable things—that God will punish me for. I fear I have lost my chance to ever see Melina and our baby again."

"The Lord God is constant with an infinite capacity to forgive, and Christ Jesus always stands ready to intercede on our behalf. You only need to seek forgiveness and atone for your sins."

"I have betrayed my faith, and Christ has turned his back on me," John declared bitterly.

"You are mistaken, my son. We may turn away from Jesus, but He never moves. He is there with his arms open, waiting for you."

John looked at the priest with desperate eyes that were welling again with tears. He asked mournfully, "What can I do to redeem myself?"

"As a Christian, you must do three things. First, you must confess your sins to God and ask his forgiveness. Second, you need to forgive yourself so that you can move forward. Lastly, you must remove yourself from the situation or environment that prompted your transgressions. Or, as our Lord said to the woman who was apprehended in the act of adultery: 'Go your way and sin no more.'"

"I don't know if I can accomplish all of that," John declared.

"God gave you free will for a reason, John Pilgrim. Your destiny is largely in your own hands," Father Sarkozy said firmly but with great gentleness.

"I deeply appreciate the time you have invested in me," John said with genuine sincerity. "Please write down instructions for getting my contributions to the church, and if you don't mind, I would like to stay here with Melina a bit longer."

"Of course, take all the time you need. I will leave a card for you on the table near the basin of holy water," Father Sarkozy said. "My heart tells me that you and Melina gave each other great joy. In times to come, remember that and try to discard the rest."

He watched the old priest totter off and noticed for the first time that he favored his left leg. He was a man who had an intimate relationship with pain, a man whose years of active, loving service had come to a close, and yet, he kept "moving forward" with faith and good cheer. It was a worthy example to follow.

John was not quite ready to speak to God, but he could talk to Melina, and so he did. He reminded her how much he loved her and missed her. He told her of the things he had done in rage to avenge her death and the loss of their child. He begged her to pardon him.

When it was time to leave, he stepped up to the little nook where the pretty urn containing Melina's ashes was perched. There was a protective glass across the alcove, and John pressed his lips against it in one final kiss.

He walked back to the nave of the church and found it empty. Father Sarkozy was somewhere else, but the card was on the little table just as he promised. John collected it and exited through the big doors from which he had entered.

He was ready now—ready to go home and deal with his situation at the CIA. No matter what happened from this point on, John knew he intended to make some fundamental changes with his life.

Chapter 15

Two days later, John arrived in Miami on a direct flight from France. He had enjoyed several visits to South Florida over the years, and he had always been attracted to the casual, yet vibrant, lifestyle of the Gold Coast and the Keys. He had considered looking for a place to live in Miami, but he really thought that Key West—the southern-most point in the continental US—was the place for him.

He had not spoken to anyone at the Company since his brief conversations with Kinsdale and Griffith, and he knew he was complicating a favorable resolution of his issues with the CIA. He also knew time was running out, and soon, he would be disavowed as a renegade operative. When that happened, an order to terminate him on sight would follow shortly thereafter. It was critical he make contact again within 24 hours.

John rented a car and hopped on US Highway 1 South to drive 160 miles to Key West. It took almost four hours, and he arrived at mid-afternoon. He checked into a motel and went apartment hunting. Two hours later, he was back at his room and thinking about having an early dinner at one of the lively restaurants in the downtown area. He tried to nap but he was too restless to relax. The images of Iran and the wounded eyes of the boy named Nabib haunted him whenever he was asleep. He strolled outside to look around.

Across the road was a boatyard with a number of vessels on stanchions. He wandered over to kill a few minutes before he booked a flight to Richmond. He fully intended to rent another car after he landed and drive in to Langley the next day. It stunned him just a little to realize he had just made that decision while standing in the doorway of his motel room.

The yard had a large repair bay with an outside storage area filled with power yachts and sailboats of all sizes and descriptions. Several of the vessels were tagged with signs offering them for sale, and more than a few of the boats were little more than derelicts. A large sloop caught his eye, and he threaded through the stands to get to it.

It was not in very good condition. The mast was up, but the mainsail hung in rags from the yard arm. It had a fiberglass hull with lots of wood topside, and all of it was covered in a patina of grime. John stepped around to the stern and noticed that the rudder had been removed. The name was faded but legible; it read *Progress, Mystic, Connecticut.*

A man came up from the direction of the shop. He was about sixty with a barrel chest and a weathered face. He wore a captain's hat set at a jaunty angle and had a checkered kerchief tied around his neck. A tuft of wiry, white chest hair sprouted above his partially unbuttoned plaid shirt. He was a walking postcard of an old sea dog.

"You picked a good one," he said. "My name is Duke Clinton, what's yours?"

"John Pilgrim. Nice to meet you, Duke," John replied as they shook hands. "I'm not in the market for a boat. I am just killing time for a bit."

"There is no charge for looking," Clinton chuckled. "Do you know sailboats, John?"

"Not so much, but I recognize this one; it is a Pearson 365, right?"

"You are dead on, man. This old gal has been here for about a month, and I have all her papers and logs all the way back to her birthday at the factory in Portsmouth, Rhode Island. Are you a sailor, John?"

"I used to be a long time ago. Small boats mostly—Sunfish and Catalina 18's. This model of the Pearson was my father's dream boat, but we were poor as church mice and never could afford one."

"You could probably swing this one. She's special; the original owner made the Great Circle with her."

"Wow! This boat has sailed around the world. She doesn't look like she could make out of the bay right now."

"You just have to look past her broken heart," Clinton said. "She has strong bones and a good soul. This boat is worthy of redemption."

"That sounds very spiritual, Duke," John replied with his eyes on the nameplate.

"Aw, don't mind me. I just love old boats, and I get carried away sometimes. You know, you could buy this one for about thirty thousand, and me and you together could bring her all the way back for another twenty and a lot of elbow grease."

"Like I said, I'm not in the market for a boat."

"Yeah, I hear you, but just so you know, I can hold that offer for only a week."

"There is no need. It was nice to meet you, but I have to get going."

"Sure thing," the old sailor said, shaking hands again. As a parting shot, he added, "You will be back, John. She has already hooked you."

The next morning John turned in his rental car at Key West International Airport and caught the earliest available flight to Richmond. Before he boarded, he called Griffith on the private cell and gave him his itinerary.

"Buzz me before you enter the reception area, so I can come up and walk you in," Griffith counseled.

"Some of these cowboys around here would love to make points by putting you in cuffs."

In Richmond, he rented another car and drove the ninety miles to CIA operations in Langley in an hour and a half. At 3:30 from the parking lot, he called the office and asked to speak to Griffith.

"I will be right up and meet you at the door," his friend said.

Griffith made sure he was cleared through security without any phone alerts to Kinsdale. They took an elevator down to the operations center.

"What gives with the dark hair and moustache? You look like a gangster."

"Just think of it as a momentary lapse in judgment."

"So what are you going to do about this mess?" Griffith asked as the car descended

"I hope to get myself cut loose, free and clear," John confided. "I appreciate what you have done for me, Adrian, more than I can say. But for now, you need to distance yourself from me. Don't get your tail in a wringer."

When the lift came to a stop, Griffith went to his desk, and John walked into Kinsdale's office without knocking.

"Well, if it isn't the prodigal son," Kinsdale said. Someone had obviously tipped him off that John was in the building. "You are in a spot of trouble, Pilgrim. You disappear for over a week; you go into a sovereign country without authorization and risk creating an international crisis. You could find yourself in prison over this little escapade."

John responded by tossing an envelope onto Kinsdale's desk. "There is my resignation, effective immediately."

His supervisor huffed, "Are you still in high school? You leave the Company only when it does not want you anymore. I already know about Dieter Heilberg—he's dead, along with a shit load of his soldiers. Now, that was a nifty piece of work, but you let Jabbar get away.

"You have had your little vacation, so I am going to send you back into the field to track down the Imam and take him out, too. After that, who knows? I had no idea you were such a good assassin."

With the same stoic reaction, John tossed another envelope on top of the first. He said, "You will want to look at this one."

Kinsdale pulled out the copy of the canceled check with the handwritten note across the bottom. His facial expression never changed.

"This means nothing," he said with confidence. "The funds were approved through the proper channels and presented to the intelligence director in Pakistan. If he misappropriated the money, I can hardly be held responsible."

John dropped a third envelope onto the desk and declared, "This one is going to be more difficult to dismiss."

Kinsdale pulled the photostat of the bank transfer report from the casing, and his face registered shock. "Where did you get this?" he seethed through clinched teeth.

"You made an off-the-books, black ops shift of fifty million bucks that ended up in the hands of a terrorist organization. The weapons they purchased with these funds have already resulted in the death of CIA operatives and have armed Jabbar's mujahidin for incursions into Afghanistan." John sat on edge of the desk so he could look down on Kinsdale. "There are six other copies of this document that I have mailed with instructions to contact the press and the Senate Intelligence Committee if anything happens to me."

"You know this is bullshit," Kinsdale protested. "The money was intended to support freedom fighters trying to overthrow the dictatorship in Syria."

"Fine. If you have a good explanation for this, let's go to the director right now," John said.

"What do want, Pilgrim?" Kinsdale relented.

"I want an acceptance, in writing, of my resignation, and I want you to expedite cashing in my 401k funds," John answered. "Have the money direct deposited to my bank account by the end of the week."

"What about these other copies floating about? When do I get them?"

"Oh, you don't get them, but you are perfectly safe so long as I don't have a fatal accident."

Thirty minutes later, John walked out of Kinsdale's office with the signed acceptance and a glowing recommendation in writing. Griffith met him near the elevator with a box.

"This came for you from the Company facility in Islamabad," he said, glancing around cautiously. "How did it go in there?"

The box had been opened and searched. It contained everything he had placed in the locker, except his gun, of course. He moved clothes aside and found his Bible in the bottom. He touched the Book with his fingers, and suddenly, he felt an urgent need to have a heart-to-heart talk with God.

"I am officially retired from the Central Intelligence Agency, Adrian. With any luck, this is the last time I will ever be in this building. Give me a little time, but I will be in touch with you, pal. I promise."

"Good grief, John! What are you going to do now?" Griffith exclaimed.

John did not hesitate with his answer. "Believe it or not, I am going to buy a boat!"

About the Author

Mitchell Medford writes thrillers and mysteries in his 1930-vintage home overlooking a deep lake in Florida.

Thank you for your readership and interest in **Pilgrim's Descent**.

You can follow the further adventures of John Pilgrim in my full length novel, **Sword of Jihad,** available on Amazon and elsewhere.

Finally, if you enjoyed the novella, I would so appreciate your review and comments at Amazon and at Goodreads. To contact me directly, visit my websites at *MitchellMedford.com* and *BlueSkyFiction.com* and let's chat.

www.ingramcontent.com/pod-product-compliance
Lightning Source LLC
Chambersburg PA
CBHW070225140626
46555CB00018B/1327